The Ghosts
in the Castle

ISBN: 1540357589
ISBN-13: 978-1540357588

Zetta Elliott

The Ghosts in the Castle

Pictures by Charity Russell

Rosetta
Press

1.

We've been in London almost a week and it still hasn't rained. If I wanted to spend my summer in a hot, crowded city, I could have stayed in Brooklyn! But Pa—my grandfather—had a stroke and Mama said he couldn't live on his own any more. So we came to London to see about moving Pa into a nursing home. They don't call it a nursing home over here, though. They call it a "care home."

Lots of things are different here—they call potato chips "crisps" and everyone drives on the opposite side of the street. But this isn't the kind of stuff I expected to see. The England I've read about in books and seen in so many movies is full of wizards, and unicorns, and magic wands. It rains every day, and kids live in castles or mansions that have secret rooms and ghosts in the attic.

Pa doesn't live in a castle—he lives in a plain brick row house in Brixton that's full of towering stacks of newspapers and hundreds of vinyl records. I haven't found any mysterious trunks or magical wardrobes in the small, stuffy rooms—and believe me, I've looked! There's nothing else to do and Mama says we have to throw out or give away all the things Pa can't take with him to the care home.

Mama and I spend most of our time in Brixton so I haven't seen much of London. I did get to ride in a red double-decker bus, so that's one thing scratched off my Important Things to Do in London list. But there's so much more I want to see and do! We haven't really had time to be tourists because Pa can't leave his bed, so mostly we just stay at home and take care of him.

I read to Pa sometimes but he usually falls asleep after just a page or two. Mama tells me to just keep on reading because what matters is that Pa knows he's not alone. I do as I'm told and hope the smile on Pa's face means he's dreaming about enchanted forests and mischievous pixies and vengeful dragons. Because of the stroke, one side of Pa's mouth droops down but he can still smile with the other side of his mouth.

My Aunt Jocelyn's coming soon, and Mama says then we'll have a chance to see more of the city. Aunt Jocelyn is Mama's younger sister. She's a professor at the University of Leicester, which is pronounced "Lester" even though that's not how it's spelled. Aunt Joss is a lot of fun. I was only five when she came to visit us in Brooklyn, but I still remember how Mama and Aunt Joss stayed up late every night. They sat at the kitchen table looking at old photographs and laughing so hard that tears rolled down their cheeks.

I also remember that they fought sometimes, too. Mama's pretty good at sucking her teeth, but Aunt Joss sucks her teeth louder and longer than anyone I know! Mama and Aunt Joss were born in England but their parents were born in Nevis. They migrated to England in the 1960s. When Mama was in college (or at "uni" as she likes to say), she left London to spend a semester

in New York City. She met Daddy at NYU and fell in love. After graduation they got married in Nevis and then bought a house in Brooklyn. So I have family in the US, the UK, and the Caribbean. Mama says it's a shame that it took Pa's stroke to bring us all together, but maybe it's a blessing in disguise since now I get to meet the rest of my cousins.

When I asked Daddy how Mama and Aunt Joss could be so happy one moment and then angry the next, he said, "Sometimes the folks you love most get so close they just rub you the wrong way." I fight with my big brother Tariq *all* the time, but not because I love him so much. We fight because he's annoying and bossy!

But Tariq doesn't get on my nerves these days because my brother didn't come to London with us. The Little League tournament is underway and Daddy thinks Tariq's team might actually win this year. If I were back in Brooklyn, I'd be cheering louder than anyone else. Tariq might be a know-it-all but he's still my big brother. And not every girl can say her brother was named MVP two years in a row!

Pa's house is quiet most of the time but all that's about to change. Aunt Joss arrives tomorrow with her son Winston. I've never met him but Mama tells me to make sure he feels welcome. Aunt Joss adopted Winston a year ago and Mama says it's important to treat him like any other member of the family.

"So I should treat Winston the way I treat Tariq?" I ask with a sneaky smile.

Mama smiles back but warns me to be on my best behavior. "Winston's had some trouble with Eustace's girls, so just be nice to him."

Eustace is my uncle and he has three daughters. I've never met them either, but Uncle Eustace sends us a family portrait every year at Christmas so I know what they look like. If a picture's worth a thousand words, I think *I* might have trouble with these girls, too. But I don't tell that to Mama. She's got too many other things to worry about right now, like taking care of Pa and making his small, cluttered house fit for the Queen!

That's what Mama calls her Aunt Pru—"Her Royal Highness" or "Her Majesty." Her real name's Prudence but Aunt Jocelyn calls her "Aunt Shrew" because she likes to criticize everyone. Aunt Pru is Pa's big sister, which makes her about a hundred years old. She lives near Leeds but she's taking the train down to London to make sure we're taking good care of her baby brother. Apparently Aunt Pru doesn't like London, but we're hosting a family dinner for her anyway. Technically she's my *great*-aunt, but the way everyone talks about Aunt Pru makes her seem like a not-so-great aunt!

2.

"Where's Useless?"

That's the first thing Aunt Joss says once she has finished hugging Mama and me. I know Aunt Joss is talking about my Uncle Eustace. He's the eldest but he doesn't have a lot of time for Pa. Uncle Eustace is a barrister (that's what they call a lawyer over here).

"Don't call him that, Joss." Mama uses her warning voice but Aunt Joss just rolls her eyes.

"You came all the way from America and got here before our brother!" she says. "Eustace lives two hours away. He should be here already."

Mama sighs and says, "Eustace will be here soon. He promised to bring the girls so they can meet Zaria." Then Mama turns her attention to me. "Why don't you take your cousin upstairs, Zaria? You and Winston will be sharing a room for the next couple of days."

I look at Winston but he doesn't look at me. He pushes his funky glasses up his nose and looks at Aunt Joss instead. When she nods at him he says, "Okay," but he still doesn't look at me.

Winston's book bag seems really heavy so I offer to help him carry it upstairs. But Winston snatches it away like I'm some kind of thief.

"I don't need any help," he says quietly.

I just shrug and say, "Suit yourself."

When we get upstairs I push the door extra hard but it still drags on the shaggy orange carpet. To my surprise, Winston leans his shoulder against the door and we manage to open it all the way.

"Thanks," I say with a smile.

Winston smiles at the floor instead of at me. "Which bed's mine?" he asks.

I point to the one against the wall and watch as Winston heaves his bag onto the bed. Then he sits down and wraps a protective arm around it.

"What you got in there?" I ask before sitting on the edge of my own bed.

Winston just looks down at his bag and mumbles, "Books."

"Really? I brought some of my favorite books with me. Want to see?"

Winston still doesn't look me in the eye but he does nod, so I quickly gather up the books stacked next to my bed and offer them to him. Winston takes them from me and carefully examines each one, smoothing down the curled up corners of the books I've read the most. He doesn't say anything while he reads the summaries written on the back.

"I like books about magic," I say, in case that isn't obvious. "What kind of books do you like?"

Winston sets my stack of books on the nightstand between our beds. Then he reaches for his bag. He unzips it and fishes around inside for one particular book. When he finally pulls it out, I'm surprised to see a unicorn on the cover!

"You have a book about unicorns?" I ask.

I reach for the book but Winston pulls it away and looks down at his shoes.

"I love unicorns," I assure him. "Can I see your book—please?"

Winston looks me in the eye for the first time. "You love unicorns?" he asks skeptically.

I nod my head and hurry on. "I even have a poster on the wall of my room. It shows a unicorn from a tapestry up at the Cloisters. That's a museum in New York filled with all kinds of medieval art."

Winston looks down at his book and then passes it to me. I read the title—*Legendary Beasts of Britain*—and ask, "What other mythical creatures do you like?"

Winston smiles shyly and says, "Gryphons are kind of cool. And I'm doing a paper for school on the Bennu bird. That's what ancient Egyptians called—"

"A phoenix!" I blurt out before Winston can finish.

"How did you know that?" he asks.

I roll my lips together and wonder what I should do. Tariq said not to tell anybody about the phoenix we found last spring. But Mama said I should treat Winston like one of the family. And you're supposed to trust your family, right?

I hop from my bed over to Winston's. "I'm going to tell you a secret—but you have to promise you won't tell anyone else."

Winston squishes up his face. "Not even my mum? I tell her everything."

I think for a moment. Aunt Joss is pretty cool—and she's

family, too. "Okay," I tell Winston, "but you can't tell anyone else. Deal?"

Winston looks down at my hand. Then he looks me in the eye, shakes my hand, and says, "Deal."

"Something awesome happened last spring. There was this abandoned building at the end of our block and the backyard was totally overgrown…"

I tell Winston everything about the phoenix on Barkley Street. We're so absorbed in our conversation that we don't notice the three girls standing in the doorway until one says, "Look who it is—Winnie the Pooh!"

The other girls snicker. Then the biggest one points at me and says, "You must be Zaria. I'm Vanessa and these are my sisters Jamila and Chantal. You can come downstairs and hang out with us now."

I look at Winston and realize he thinks I'm actually going to go with them. I hand him the unicorn book and say, "Here, hold this for a minute."

Winston takes the book from me and shoves it back inside his bag so the three girls can't see it.

Vanessa turns to go. "Come on," she says impatiently. "You don't have to stay up here with fairy boy."

"Don't call him that," I say angrily.

Vanessa puts her hand on her hip and turns back to face me. "He's not really our cousin, you know. He's adopted."

"So what?" I say with enough attitude to make Vanessa step back into the room.

"So…that means I can talk to him any way I like," she says in a super snooty voice.

Winston's been looking at the floor this whole time. I put my arm around him and pull him close so he knows I've got his back.

"Well, he's my cousin *and* my friend. He's not bothering you so why don't you just leave him alone?"

"Why don't you make me?" Vanessa says.

Jamila and Chantal both go, "Oooooh!" and step back so Vanessa has more room. I put on my low-down-mean-and-nasty look and get up from the bed.

I put my hands on my hips and say, "You do know I'm from Brooklyn, right?"

"We know all about you. We thought you'd be cool." Vanessa looks me up and down and snickers. "But looks like you're a geek—just like him!"

I take one step toward Vanessa and she takes one step back. I've never started a fight with a girl but I've learned how to stand up to my brother—and Tariq is bigger than this mean-mouthed girl. If he were here now, it'd be three against three. But Tariq can't have my back when he's still in Brooklyn, so I'm going to have to handle this myself.

I take my earrings off and hand them to Winston. "Hold these for me," I tell him. They're tiny gold hoops but taking them off lets Vanessa know that I'm ready to fight *hard*.

Vanessa puffs out her chest and says, "You don't scare me," but I can tell she's lying. She *is* scared. Her sisters look like they're ready to run back downstairs.

I take another step forward and tell her, "In Brooklyn we say, 'Don't start nothing, won't be nothing.' You sure you want to start

EDDy GRANT

something with me?"

Vanessa looks from me to Winston and then back at me. Suddenly we hear the heavy thud of adult feet coming up the stairs. Mama appears in the hallway, takes one look at me and asks, "What's going on in here?"

I look at Vanessa and wait for her to answer either my question or Mama's. She looks me up and down before turning to my mother with a sweet smile on her face.

"Nothing, Aunt Dorette. We were just wondering if you needed any help in the kitchen."

Mama puts her arm around Vanessa's shoulder and ushers her out of the bedroom. "That sounds like an excellent idea. Why don't you girls come back downstairs with me?"

As soon as Mama leaves with the three nasty girls, Aunt Joss pokes her head around the doorframe. She looks at Winston but I know her question is for me. "Everything okay in here?"

I sit back down on the bed next to my cousin. "Everything's fine, Aunt Joss," I say with a smile.

Winston beams at me before nodding at his mother. Then he hands me back my earrings and hauls the heavy book bag onto his lap so he can show me the rest of his books. Aunt Joss winks at me before going back downstairs, and Winston tells me everything he has found out about the phoenix of ancient Egypt.

3.

After Mama went to all that trouble for "Her Majesty," Aunt Pru doesn't even come to our family dinner. She calls to say she'll be dining with friends instead, and though Mama pretends to be disappointed, she looks a lot more relaxed once she knows Aunt Pru isn't on her way over.

When I ask if Winston and I can take our plates up to our room, Aunt Joss kisses the top of my head and whispers, "Thank you, sweetheart" in my ear.

She doesn't have to thank me. Hanging out with Winston is a LOT of fun! He knows even more about magic than I do. I have to put my plate down more than once so I can get my notebook and write down some of the amazing things he's telling me. At the end of the night, when everyone else has gone home, Winston asks his "mum" if they can give me a proper tour of London tomorrow.

"Of course," Aunt Joss says.

"That's an excellent idea," Mama adds. "I'll stay here with Pa."

"No, you won't," says Aunt Joss. "You need a little holiday, too. Eustace is useless but maybe Mrs. Lawson could stay with Pa for a few hours."

The kettle starts to whistle on the stove, so Mama gets up to make the tea. At home Mama drinks coffee, but here in London she drinks cups and cups and cups of tea!

"You two should get ready for bed," Mama says. "Unless you'd like some Horlicks."

I look at Winston to see if we should say yes. I don't know what Horlicks is, but Winston shakes his head so hard I know it must be gross.

"Uh—no thanks, Mama. We'll just go to bed."

"You both need a bath first," Aunt Joss says. She puts a hand on Winston's head and steers him out of the kitchen. "Starting with you, sir."

I'm about to follow them upstairs when Mama says, "Just a minute, Zaria."

I turn around and watch Mama as she takes a sip from her mug of tea. It's hot here in London and it's hot in this house, but Mama insists that drinking hot tea cools her body down. I can hear the water running upstairs and bet Winston's taking a cold bath. That's what I plan to do!

Mama's watching me but she's not saying anything. "What is it, Mama?" I ask.

She takes another sip of tea before setting her mug down on the counter. "Aunt Pru wants to take you out for tea."

When we arrived on Sunday, Mama made us a meal from the few items of food in Pa's kitchen. That night I learned that sometimes "tea" means a hot drink, and sometimes it means "supper." I think about that first meal in London and frown. "Aunt Pru wants to take me out for beans on toast?"

Mama laughs. "No. Having high tea at Kensington Palace

means eating dainty cucumber sandwiches and scones with jam and clotted cream."

Suddenly having tea at a palace with Her Royal Highness doesn't sound so bad! But something still doesn't seem right. "Why me?" I ask.

Mama shrugs. "I don't know. But it's awfully nice of her to invite you, right?"

I think for a moment. Is it "nice" to have tea with someone who isn't very nice? I'd like to see Kensington Palace but I'm not sure I want to go there alone with "Aunt Shrew."

"Can Winston come?" I ask Mama.

She shakes her head. "Aunt Pru only invited you."

"That's not fair," I reply. "Winston's part of the family, too."

"So are Vanessa, Jamila, and Chantal, but Aunt Pru didn't invite them."

Thank goodness, I think to myself. Out loud I say, "What's so special about me?"

Mama wraps her arms around me and gives me a squeeze. "Where should I start? You're kind, and clever, and the best bowler in Brooklyn. Maybe Aunt Pru just wants to get to know her grand-niece from America."

I squeeze Mama back and ask, "Why can't Winston come, too?"

"It didn't take long for you two to become friends," Mama says.

"I'm glad Winston's here," I tell Mama. "Don't tell Tariq, but I kind of miss having a brother."

Mama laughs and promises she won't tell Tariq that I miss

him. Then Aunt Joss comes downstairs and says, "The bathroom's all yours, Zaria."

I leave Mama and Aunt Joss in the kitchen but linger on the stairs so I can hear what they say next. It's not polite to eavesdrop but grown-ups say some interesting stuff when they think kids aren't around.

"Did you tell her?"

Mama must nod because Aunt Joss asks another question. "What are you going to do about her hair?"

I reach up and stroke one of my Afro puffs. Why would Mama do anything to my hair?

Then I hear Mama say, "She's never worn it straight."

Aunt Joss pulls a chair out from the table. I hear the air wheeze out of the vinyl cushion as she plunks down. "She's got good, thick hair. We could try a home perm."

"No!" Mama says in a sharp voice that makes me jump. "We'll just press it."

Aunt Joss laughs and says, "Ma's hot comb is probably still in the drawer next to the stove! All you need is some grease."

Mama's voice sounds funny—like she's sad and angry at the same time. "Whatever we do will be temporary. I'm sure Aunt Pru will be satisfied so long as Zaria looks nice and neat."

"She'll have to wear a dress," Aunt Joss says.

I can't see what Mama does next but after a few seconds, she and Aunt Joss bust out laughing. I don't really wear dresses and I didn't bring any with me to London. That means we'll have to go shopping, and I HATE shopping. I quietly climb the stairs and head for the bathroom. While the tub is filling up with cool water,

I look at my reflection in the mirror. I don't see anything wrong with my hair, and it always does look "nice and neat"—at least it looks that way to me.

I think about Aunt Pru's invitation while I'm having my bath. By the time I pull on my pajamas and slip into bed, I've decided I won't be having tea with the Queen. I'd rather stay here in Pa's stuffy house and have beans on toast with Winston.

4.

When Winston and I wake up the next day, the sun is shining through our bedroom window—again.

I groan into my pillow. Then I sit up and look at Winston. "When's it going to rain?" I ask him.

Winston yawns and gives me a funny look. "You *want* it to rain?"

"It's *supposed* to rain in England," I tell him. "It's so hot here, I feel like I'm back in Brooklyn!"

By lunchtime, I'm wishing that I really was at home again. It's fun riding "the Tube" around the city—the London Underground is a lot cleaner and quieter than the New York City subway. And Winston tells me lots of cool stuff about the gargoyles perched on top of some really old buildings. But no matter where we go, Mama and Aunt Joss can't seem to agree on anything!

It starts before we even leave the house. The first argument is about what to make for breakfast. Aunt Joss wants to make us a full English breakfast: fried bread, grilled tomatoes, baked beans, mushrooms, poached eggs, black pudding, bacon, and sausages (which they call "bangers")! But to do a "fry-up," Aunt Joss would have to go to the grocery store and Mama says we don't have time. Mama thinks we should just have cereal for breakfast and get fish and chips for lunch. Winston and I don't really care—we just want to get going!

Next Mama and Aunt Joss bicker about how much to pay Mrs. Lawson. She's the nice lady who lives next door. She's willing to stay with Pa for free, but Mama says we ought to pay her for her time. Aunt Joss says that will insult Mrs. Lawson who just wants to be a good neighbor. When we finally leave the house and start our big tour, Mama keeps checking her watch and that makes Aunt Joss mad. Mama feels guilty and thinks we should hurry back to Pa, but Aunt Joss says he's in good hands and would want us to make the most of our day out.

The next thing Mama and Aunt Joss fight about is where we should go first. Mama wants us to go to the Museum of Natural History, but Aunt Joss says there's a new exhibit at the V&A. Winston explains that's short for the Victoria and Albert Museum. Queen Victoria ruled England for a really long time and Prince Albert was her husband, but he died when he was still a young man. Winston says Queen Elizabeth has been monarch even longer than Victoria and when she's in London, she stays at Buckingham Palace. That's on my list!

I consider showing Mama and Aunt Joss my Important Things to Do in London list, but I'm not sure they really care about what I *want* to see. Mama and Aunt Joss are more concerned with what I *should* see. I show my list to Winston instead. He looks it over carefully and says the Tower of London is more interesting than Buckingham Palace.

"It's a medieval castle and the Crown Jewels are kept there. There's no water in the moat," Winston warns me, "but it's right on the River Thames, not far from London Bridge."

London Bridge is also on my list! I decide to ask Mama if we can go where *I* want to go today, but she and Aunt Joss are busy arguing over a colorful tourist map. Mama and Aunt Joss have one thing in common: when they're mad, their Caribbean accent gets stronger and their voices get louder. When Aunt Joss sucks her teeth and grabs the map out of Mama's hands, I see my chance and tug at Mama's arm.

"Can we go see the Tower of London?" I ask.

Aunt Joss lowers the map so I can see the smile on her face. "That's an excellent idea, Zaria!"

Mama frowns. "Don't you want to see the dinosaur fossils at the Natural History Museum? That used to be my favorite place to go when I was your age."

Aunt Joss rolls her eyes and buries her face in the map once more. I look at Mama and smile while folding up my list. I shove it in my back pocket and say, "Sure, Mama. Let's go!"

There are lots of tourists waiting to enter the Natural History Museum, but the line moves quickly and before long we're inside. Most museums are free in London, so we don't have to pay. We spend hours looking at all the specimens preserved long ago by British scientists. But Mama says the museum doesn't feel the same without "Dippy."

Aunt Joss rolls her eyes and says, "You've been gone a long time, Dorette. Things do change, you know!"

I think the massive skeleton of the blue whale is just as cool as any dinosaur, but I don't tell Mama that.

Winston informs me that "Dippy"—the super long dinosaur

fossil that used to be in the museum's main hall—was actually from the US.

"Dippy's American?" I ask.

Winston nods. "It was just a plaster-cast model but still quite impressive. Dippy's scientific name is *Diplodocus carnegii*."

Aunt Joss grunts. "Imagine naming a dinosaur after yourself! 'Dippy' was a gift from Andrew Carnegie, one of your infamous American robber barons."

"Carnegie was born in Scotland," Winston reminds his mother.

I'm about to ask Aunt Joss what a robber baron is when Mama grabs my hand and announces, "Time for lunch!"

We find the exit and are swept outside by the same stream of tourists that swept us in. Mama looks at her watch—again—and says we might as well visit the V&A next since it's right across the street. I smother a groan. I don't want to visit another museum!

"When are we going to visit a castle?" I ask in my most respectful voice. Mama doesn't like it when I whine, and I know I'm starting to sound like a broken record. But I wouldn't have to keep asking the same question if Mama and Aunt Joss would just listen to me.

Suddenly Aunt Joss stops walking and tilts her ear up to the sky. The rest of us stop as well, forcing the river of people to flow around us. Some people look annoyed and others glance back to see what's wrong with Aunt Joss. I sort of wish the river would sweep me away from my embarrassing family, but Mama holds onto my hand and anchors me in the street. She doesn't ask her sister what's wrong. Instead Mama tilts her head as well and then turns in the direction of the music that's floating above our heads like bubbles.

A man with long dreadlocks is playing the steel drum on the sidewalk. He smiles and bops as he lightly beats the two shiny metal bowls, making them ring like bells under the sea. Before long Mama and Aunt Joss are bopping and smiling, too. Winston reaches into his pocket and pulls out a gold pound coin. I was going to save my fancy gold two-pound coin to take back to Brooklyn, but instead I follow Winston over to the busker and drop it into the bucket on the ground. The man winks at me and keeps on playing.

Aunt Joss sighs contentedly and links her arm through Mama's. "Ready to go?"

Mama nods and reaches for my hand. "Let's grab a quick bite and head to the Tower of London."

I beam at Mama and mentally scratch "visit a castle" off my Important Things to Do in London list!

Technically, the Tower of London *is* a castle. But like Winston said, it doesn't have a moat any more—just a grassy ditch where water used to be. Plus it's in the middle of London. It *is* old but it doesn't *feel* old when there are buses and cars whizzing by right outside the Tower gate. At least there's a drawbridge!

Winston shares cool facts about the ravens that live at the Tower. There have to be six or legend says that the kingdom and the Tower will fall! Winston also tells me that for hundreds of years they also used to keep exotic animals in the Royal Menagerie.

"There were grizzly bears and alligators from the Americas, kangaroos from Australia, tigers from Asia, and lions from Africa.

But in 1832 the Duke of Wellington sent the last of the animals to the London Zoo," Winston explains.

Aunt Joss overhears him and joins the conversation. "Yes—it only took them six hundred years to realize that making frightened animals fight to the death was cruel."

Mama jabs Aunt Joss in the ribs with her elbow and our tour of the Tower of London begins.

For a little while, everything's okay. Our tour guide is called a Beefeater. He lives at the Tower and wears the funny red and gold outfit of the Royal Bodyguards. He tells us gruesome tales of the people who were tortured here in the past. Then the Beefeater talks about Henry VIII and his six wives. We even see the spot where Ann Boleyn was beheaded! But when the Beefeater cracks a joke about sometimes wanting to do the same thing to his own wife, the smile slides off Aunt Joss' face. She mutters something about "misogyny" and turns Winston away before he has a chance to tip the man.

The best part is seeing the sparkling gems that decorate the crowns, orbs, and scepters used by the Royal Family. We stand in a long line that snakes past glass cases filled with the Crown Jewels. It's clear that Aunt Joss is in a sour mood again because she says in a loud voice that it's "pure cheek" to have a donation box on the wall when the priceless diamonds, and emeralds, and rubies have been stolen from Africa and Asia by the British.

"How does the robber ask the robbed to pay for his loot?" my aunt asks no one in particular.

A freckled boy in line behind us hears Aunt Joss and asks his father if the jewels really were stolen by the Queen. The boy's father turns red and tells his son that Britain used to own a bunch of different countries and the jewels were a gift.

Aunt Joss laughs out loud and turns to the little red-headed boy. "If I invite you into my house, you are a guest. Right?"

The boy nods and Aunt Joss continues. "If I don't invite you into my house—if you *break* into my house—what does that make you?"

"A burglar!" cries the boy, proud to know the right answer.

His red-faced father drags the boy away before Aunt Joss can start telling him all about "the evil Empire." Mama sighs as Aunt Joss instead tells me about how the British invaded other people's countries and took home all the valuable things they found. "British museums are full of artifacts that are stolen from around the world," she says in a sad, solemn voice.

Aunt Joss points to a giant diamond set in an elaborate crown that has fur trim and purple velvet. "That's the Koh-i-Noor diamond," she tells me. "India wants it back but the British government refuses to hand it over." She points to another enormous diamond at the top of a scepter. "And that's the Star of Africa." Aunt Joss sucks her teeth and says, "These are the original blood diamonds. They called *us* 'savages,' but is that really how 'civilized' people act?"

I wonder if this is the sort of thing I'll learn about when I go to "uni." Judging by the look on Winston's face, he's heard this lecture before. He looks sort of embarrassed but I can tell he's also proud of his mother.

I'm kind of interested in what Aunt Joss is saying, but it's clear that Mama's had enough.

DONATION
Box
rooklyn

"Alright, Joss," she says in a voice that doesn't hide how annoyed she is. "Let's finish up the tour—without the social commentary."

When we get outside I pull out my list. "That wasn't a proper castle," I tell Winston. "It's too small."

"It's more of a fortress, really," Winston says.

"So now you're an expert on medieval architecture, huh?" Aunt Joss sounds stern but I see the twinkle in her eye.

"Castles are supposed to be…." I pause to search for the right word.

"Majestic," Winston says.

"Exactly!" I cry. "Fit for a king—or queen."

"Someone has been reading too many fairy tales, I think," Aunt Joss says with a smile.

"Fairy tales are for little kids," I tell her. "The books I read are *much* better."

"Are they?" Aunt Joss asks. "The kids having amazing adventures in your beloved books—do they look like you?"

"What do you mean?" I ask even though I can see Winston warning me with his eyes to keep quiet.

"Here's what I mean," Aunt Joss says. "You love books about castles and wizards and magical creatures, but *you* are not in those books. The hero is always White."

Mama frowns. "That's enough, Joss. She's just a child."

Aunt Joss puts her arm around Winston. "That's when it starts, Dorette. I can't believe you let Zaria fill her head with the same nonsense they fed us when we were kids—Enid Blyton and E. Nesbit and C.S. Lewis. I would never let Winston read that clap trap!"

I look at Winston and wonder if his mother knows about all the books he's got stashed in his book bag. I try to ask him with my eyes but Winston's staring at the ground.

"Why don't you worry about your child and let me worry about mine?" Mama suggests in a not-so-nice voice.

Before Aunt Joss can reply, Mama wraps a protective arm around my shoulder and leads me away from the Tower of London. "We'll see you back at Pa's," Mama says just in case Aunt Joss was thinking about following us.

I look over my shoulder at Winston. He waves at me and shrugs like this sort of thing happens all the time.

Soon the busy street we're walking along runs into two others. There's a concrete island in the middle of the three streets. A large tree shades three stone benches. Mama says, "Let's sit here for a while."

It is hot but I'm not all that tired, and what I really want is to go back to Winston and Aunt Joss. I think Mama needs a time out, though, so I nod and we cross the street to the triangular island. For a while we sit on the cool stone bench without saying anything. Cars zip by but traffic isn't as noisy here as it is in New York. Hardly any cars honk their horn and I haven't heard a single siren!

Mama surprises me by suddenly asking, "Do you like it here, Zaria? Do you like London?"

"Sure," I say. "There are lots of cool things to see—and lots of history. London feels old and new at the same time."

Mama nods but keeps her eyes on the cars whizzing by.

"Would you like to live here—maybe go to school and learn more about Britain's history?"

Surprise sends my eyebrows up to the sky. "Are we moving to London, Mama?"

Mama puts her arm around me and gives me a squeeze. "No, baby, we're not. It's just that...well, you know Aunt Pru wants to take you to tea this week. She also wants to give you a gift."

"Really?"

"Not like a birthday present. It's more like—an advantage."

I crumple up my eyebrows and think hard for a moment. "How do you give someone an advantage?" I ask.

Mama takes a deep breath. Then she says, "Sometimes an opportunity comes along and it's only offered to certain people—like going to a really good school. An excellent education would give you an advantage."

"I already go to a really good school in Brooklyn," I remind her.

Mama smiles but her face doesn't look happy at all. "This school is different. It's a prestigious boarding school out in the country. You know what a boarding school is, right?"

My eyes open wide. I know *exactly* what a boarding school is. All the characters in my favorite books attend boarding school! They wear fancy uniforms with a crest, and live in dormitories with quirky roommates, and eat their meals in a dining hall that looks like a cathedral.

Mama squeezes my hand and says, "Let's just think about it for a while, okay?"

I nod and let Mama pull me to my feet.

"We better go home and check on Pa," she says.

As we head toward the Tube station, I think about what it would be like to live in England. "Would Winston go to boarding school with me?" I ask Mama.

She presses her lips together and shakes her head.

"What about Vanessa, Jamila, and Chantal—will they be at this school?" I ask, hoping the answer will be "no."

Mama shakes her head again. "Only you, Zaria. Aunt Pru chose you."

I should feel relieved but instead I feel a little bit queasy. There are eccentric old ladies in the books that I've read, and sometimes orphans inherit money from a relative they've never even met. But I'm not an orphan. So why did Aunt Pru choose me?

5.

When I wake up the next morning, the sun isn't shining. I jump up on the bed and look out the window. The pavement is still dry but the sky is filled with ominous grey clouds.

"Rain!" I whisper to myself before bouncing back into bed.

Winston opens his eyes and laughs at me. "I have a surprise for you," he says.

"Did you cast a spell to make it rain?" I ask.

Winston smiles mischievously but shakes his head. "We're going to Windsor Castle today! That's where the Queen lives when she's not in London. You'll love it—it's a proper castle. It's almost a thousand years old!"

Once we're dressed, Winston and I head downstairs for breakfast. Aunt Joss is standing at the stove and Mama is sitting at the table sipping a cup of tea. They don't look like they've been arguing, and whatever Aunt Joss is cooking smells delicious.

"Take a seat, if you please," she says cheerfully, "and prepare your bellies for a full English breakfast!"

Aunt Joss sets two plates on the table. The only time I've seen this much food piled on my plate is at Thanksgiving. I grab my fork and dig in. Winston does the same. Aunt Joss hands a smaller plate to Mama who takes it upstairs to Pa.

"If he'd rather have cornmeal porridge, just let me know,"

Aunt Joss calls after her.

"He might like a change," Mama says as she heads upstairs. "It sure does smell good."

Aunt Joss smiles with pride as she watches us eat. "It's so nice having our family together like this."

I bite into a banger and think about how great it would be to see Aunt Joss and Winston more often. I could definitely get used to eating this kind of food! But then I remember that we're selling Pa's house and if I went to boarding school, I wouldn't get to have breakfast with Winston and Aunt Joss every day. I could spend holidays with them—unless I went back to Brooklyn. To my surprise, I suddenly wish my big brother were here. I don't usually ask Tariq for advice, but I'd like to know what he would do if he were in my shoes.

Mrs. Lawson rings the doorbell before letting herself into the house. Mama gave her a set of keys yesterday so she can come and go while we're out of the house. Aunt Joss makes Mrs. Lawson a cup of tea and they sit at the kitchen table while Winston and I wash the dishes. Mrs. Lawson says she's sure Pa's house will sell quickly. When Aunt Joss grunts, I look at Winston and wonder if Mrs. Lawson's about to get a long lecture on real estate.

But Aunt Joss just sips her tea and says, "Good ol' gentrification."

"Everybody wants to live in Brixton these days," Mrs. Lawson says. "It's not like it was when your ma and pa moved here decades ago. There are so many new shops, so many new faces. I hardly recognize the old neighborhood!"

Before Aunt Joss can reply, Mama comes into the kitchen and

asks, "Ready to go?"

We pile into Aunt Joss's car and head for Windsor. England looks very ordinary from the highway but soon we leave the city behind and there—perched on a hill in the distance—is Windsor Castle!

Now THIS is a castle! There are turrets and above the castle's large, round tower the Union Jack is flapping in the wind, which means the Queen isn't at home. I have a feeling something magical is going to happen here!

We queue (line up) for our tickets and go through security just like we did at the airport. Then we go outside and head for the north terrace where we'll find the entrance to the castle. Even though there are lots of tourists walking around snapping photos with selfie sticks, it feels like we've gone back in time. The grey stone walls that ring the castle are made of uneven bricks that were clearly made by hand, and there are hideous gargoyles snarling and leering above every stone arch we pass through. Dark clouds loom overhead, though rain still hasn't started to fall.

Winston points at one of the black lamps attached to the stone wall and I see that there's a small gold crown at the very top. In the old days before electricity, the lamps would have held a candle instead of a light bulb. I close my eyes for a moment and imagine myself walking along this same stone pathway by candlelight. Then I think about what Aunt Joss said about the characters in my books not looking like me. I open my eyes and frown. Were there girls like me who lived in castles like this? I'm not sure.

Mama puts her arm around my shoulder and pulls me back

into the present.

"What do you think?" she asks. "Is this a *real* castle?"

I banish my doubts and beam up at her. "It's perfect, Mama!"

Like the Tower of London, the moat at Windsor Castle is dry. Without any water in it, the moat is more of a lush green valley. It's been turned into a pretty garden with a red brick walkway and a fountain. We pass a door that leads down to the moat garden but it's marked PRIVATE. Most tourists just stream on by, eager to get inside the castle.

"Let's take a picture," Aunt Joss suggests.

Mama, Winston, and I line up along the stone wall and smile as the flash goes off. I blink away the white spots floating in front of my eyes and peer over the moat wall one last time before moving on. To my surprise, in the green valley below I see a boy! His skin is brown like mine and his hair is braided across his head in a way I've never seen before. The boy wears a long white robe that trails after him as he walks, and around his neck is a fancy silver necklace.

I watch as he kneels down and dips his fingers in the fountain. He seems to sigh as he looks at his reflection in the dark pool of water. Then he pads across the plush grass with his bare feet and climbs the stone steps that lead up to the castle.

I want to call out to the boy but instead I search for Winston. He'll know who this boy is! He must be special to have access to places that are off-limits for the rest of us.

Winston, Mama, and Aunt Joss are heading for the north terrace. Winston turns back and waves at me to come on. I point to the moat but Winston turns and keeps on walking up the stone

path.

I look down into the green valley. There are so many shrubs and flowers growing alongside the stone steps that for a moment I can't find the boy. Then I see a flash of white—there he is! I watch in amazement as the boy opens a narrow gate marked PRIVATE and then walks *straight through* a closed wooden door!

I rub my eyes and scan the lush garden for signs of the boy. Maybe he ducked behind a bush, I tell myself. He couldn't have walked through a closed door. Unless...*unless*...

I think about all the ghost stories I've read. In my books, dead people can do things that live people can't—and ghosts often linger in places that matter to them. But why would there be a dead Black boy wandering around Windsor castle?

Part of me thinks I'm letting my imagination run away with me. But another part of me *knows* this boy has a story to tell, and I think he wants to tell it to me! I race to catch up with Winston, Mama, and Aunt Joss. I run so hard that I can barely speak when I find them standing at the end of a very long line.

"There you are," says Mama. "Are you ready to go inside?"

I put my hands on my knees and try to stop panting so I can tell Winston about the mysterious boy. "You won't believe...what I just saw..."

Winston just grins and says, "Nothing outside the castle can compare to what you'll see *inside*."

I grab hold of Winston's arm. "But I saw a—there was a boy...and he...he disappeared!"

Suddenly I realize that Winston's not the only one looking at me. Mama and Aunt Joss are listening and so are other people standing in line. I lower my voice and mumble, "I'll tell you later."

Winston nods but gives me a funny look. Aunt Joss frowns and looks at her watch.

"This queue is ridiculous," she says impatiently. "We'll be here for hours!"

"Everyone wants to see Queen Mary's Dolls' House," Mama says, looking at me hopefully. "Do you want to start there, Zaria?"

I'm not sure why they call it a dolls' house over here, but I guess it's for the same reason they say "maths" instead of "math." I can tell Mama really wants me to see the dolls' house with her but I am finally at a real castle—and I think I just saw a ghost! The last thing I want to do is look at a bunch of dolls.

Aunt Joss rolls her eyes at Mama so I don't have to. "The girl wants to see the *castle*, Dorette."

Mama looks disappointed until Winston tugs her hand and says, "I'll go see the dolls' house with you, Auntie."

Aunt Joss gives Winston a sweet smile—and so do I.

"Right! You and Winston stay here and queue," she suggests, "and I'll take Zaria through the State Apartments. There's no queue for that tour, so we won't be long."

Mama agrees. "We can meet by the chapel afterward and watch the changing of the guard."

I wave to Winston as we walk away. When Mama can't see, I throw my arms around Aunt Joss and give her a squeeze. I'd rather tour the castle with Winston, but I appreciate him and Aunt Joss saving me from the dolls' house. It's hard traveling with adults! The next time I see the solitary boy, I'm going to ask him how he got permission from his mother to roam the castle on his own.

It's quiet in the State Apartments because most of the tourists are listening to the audio guide. With their ears covered by headphones, they walk through the spacious rooms wearing a look of awe. When we pass a giant mirror that stretches from the floor to the ceiling, I realize that I have that same look on my face, too!

Everything is covered in gold! There are rooms that are red and rooms that are green. There is a wall covered with several circles of antique guns and in the center is a golden unicorn's head. There are suits of armor and a knight seated on a horse. There are cases containing the armor worn by leaders from other countries who were defeated in battle. Aunt Joss looks like there's a lot she wants to say, but for now she keeps her lips sealed.

Red ropes keep visitors from getting too close to the priceless furnishings. We pass through a room full of china in glass cases. I think about the times I've watched *Antiques Roadshow* and how one plate sometimes turns out to be worth a thousand dollars. There are too many plates here to count! In another glass case there are white porcelain figurines of people from Asia. On one marble mantelpiece there is a golden sculpture that shows a man with ink-black skin smiling and wearing a turban.

"You see that, right?" Aunt Joss asks irritably. I nod but don't hear the lecture she starts to deliver because suddenly I see the boy!

He looks different this time but it's definitely the same boy. Instead of a loose white robe he wears a grey woolen suit with socks and shoes. His braids are gone and now his hair is cut close to his head. In his hand he holds a boater—a straw hat with a flat top and striped band. In the books I've read, kids who attend boarding school sometimes wear a boater as part of their summer uniform. Does that mean the boy attends a private school (which they call a public school over here)? He still looks lonely—and bored—but he also seems a bit older than he was when I saw him before. That was just twenty minutes ago—how could he have aged so quickly?

I realize my mouth is hanging open, so I pull up my lip and glance at Aunt Joss. She's pointing but not at the boy. Aunt Joss is talking about the black-faced sculpture as if she doesn't even see the Black boy standing right beneath it! I watch as he runs his small brown fingers along the smooth marble mantelpiece before shivering and staring at the empty grate as if he wished a blazing fire burned there.

I open my mouth once more. What should I say? Can he even hear me? I clear my throat and ask, "Are you cold?"

Without turning around, the boy replies, "I'm always cold in this country." He coughs and looks past me out the tall windows that line the wall. "It never stops raining here."

I spin around and look outside, too. He's right! Raindrops streak down the glass, blurring the world outside. I grin from ear to ear. It's raining, I'm in a haunted castle in England, and the ghost that no one else can see is talking to me! I just *knew* something magical was going to happen today.

Aunt Joss has stopped lecturing and is moving on to the next room. I quickly come up with an excuse to stay and talk to the boy.

"Uh—you go ahead, Aunt Joss. I'm going to make some quick sketches." I make a show of pulling my notebook out of my book bag. Cameras aren't allowed inside the castle so my excuse actually makes sense. Aunt Joss nods and says she'll wait for me in the next room.

Once she's gone, I get as close to the boy as I can without touching the rope that separates the visitor walkway from the furnishings in the room. I open my notebook and pretend to be drawing the weird sculpture on the mantelpiece.

"So," I begin, "do you live here at the castle?"

The boy shakes his head before flopping onto a fancy divan. He tosses his boater across the room like a frisbee. I look around but no one else seems to have noticed—not even the castle wardens who are in every room and keep a close eye on visitors.

"Where are you from?" I ask the boy. "I saw you in the garden earlier but you were wearing different clothes." If other people can hear me, they don't seem to mind that I'm talking to myself!

The boy crosses his ankles and folds his arms behind his head. "Where are you from?" he asks.

"Brooklyn," I answer then think to add, "That's a borough in New York City."

He sweeps his eyes over me and asks, "Are you American then?"

"African American," I say.

The boy hops off the divan and looks at me like I just became much more interesting. "You're African?" he asks.

"*African American*," I explain. "My ancestors came from Africa but I was born in the United States."

"Oh," he says with obvious disappointment. "I thought perhaps you were…"

The boy turns away and wanders over to the far corner of the room. I don't want him to vanish again so I try to keep him talking.

"Yes?"

He sighs again and says, "Never mind. I have to go now."

"Wait!" I cry. "My name is Zaria. What's your name?"

The boy turns to face me, lifts his chin, and proudly proclaims, "I am Prince Alemayehu, son of Emperor Tewodros II and Empress Tiruwork Wube of Abyssinia."

I know there are lots of countries in Africa—more than there are states in the Union—but I don't know of any country named Abyssinia. I've also never met a prince before, so I'm not sure what to say or do. But the prince seems to be waiting for me to do *something* so…I bow.

"You may attend me, if you wish," he says with a wave of his hand.

"I'd like to but…I can't go in there," I say.

"Why not?" the prince asks in his careless way.

I point to the rope hanging between us. "These apartments are off limits to tourists," I tell him.

"You are my guest—no one would dare stop you," he says in a voice that makes me think he's used to having people follow his commands.

I glance around the room. The tourists with their handsets and headphones don't seem to be paying attention to either of us. I put my notebook back inside my bag. Then I place one hand on the red rope. The castle warden is looking right at me but she doesn't say a word as I swing my leg over the rope and step onto the plush carpet. Perhaps the prince really can protect me. Whatever makes him invisible to everyone else seems to be making me invisible, too!

"This way," he says, heading over to a corner of the room. I don't see a door and wonder if we'll both be able to glide through the wall.

I scurry across the room and pick up the prince's boater first. When I hand it to him he accepts the hat with a silent nod and then reaches up to press his fingers against the embossed wallpaper. Before I can ask him what he's doing, a door in the wall pops open—a door with no knob and no frame. A secret door!

"Do you live here?" I ask. "You seem to know the castle really well."

The prince shrugs and I think I see tears shining in his dark eyes. "I don't live anywhere—not any more." Then he nods at the never-ending stream of tourists flowing by on the other side of the rope. "They don't even see me—but *you* do."

For the first time, the prince smiles. "I can go anywhere I want," he says as he pulls open the secret door. "Well, almost anywhere."

"Where *can't* you go," I ask.

"Home," says the prince in a wistful voice.

Then he walks through the secret door and waits for me to pass through before pulling it shut behind us.

6.

I follow the prince down a narrow, shadowy corridor. It's hard to see in the dark so I reach out and place my hand on his shoulder. I'm not sure if you're supposed to touch royalty like that, but the prince doesn't seem to mind. He stops after a few minutes and runs his fingers along a wooden beam. A sliver of light enters the corridor as another secret door opens, letting us into a spacious room that has no red rope and no tourists.

"These are the Queen's private chambers," the prince explains. "No one will bother us here."

To my surprise, he races across the room and launches himself onto a satiny striped sofa covered with embroidered cushions. He tosses a small round cushion at me and points to the sofa directly across from the one he pounced on. "Your turn!" he cries with glee.

Even though there's no one around to see me, I don't feel right bouncing on the couch like I would if I were at home. The furniture in this room seems more modern than the fancy, fussy antiques in the State Apartments. The room is still majestic, though, with the same high ceilings and tall windows that line the wall. It's still raining so not much light comes in, and the large empty room feels a bit chilly.

I hear a soft voice singing a song in a language I don't know. The prince hears it too and frowns.

"Oh, no!" he whines. "It's *her*. She must have come back again."

I look around the room but don't see anyone. "Who's come back?"

"Sally," he says with a sneer. The prince hops off his sofa, pushes aside a few cushions on mine, and sits down next to me. He leans in and whispers, "That's not her real name but that's what they call her."

I listen as the voice grows louder. Before long I see a movement over by the window. The heavy brocade curtains stir and a cold draft makes me shiver. I go over to the window to see if someone left it open but it is sealed tight. I push the curtain aside and gasp when I find a small girl in a fancy dress perched on the window seat.

"Are you Sally?" I ask.

She nods and keeps on singing her strange song.

"Do you live here, too?"

The girl stops singing and smoothes out her silk skirt. "No, but today I have an audience with the Queen," she says proudly.

The prince laughs as he joins us at the window. "Sally loves to dance for the Queen. She's like a monkey in the circus." The prince tickles his own ribs and hops around as if he's a chimpanzee.

Sally jumps up and hisses at the prince, "Saucy boy!" Then she calms herself and links her arm through mine. She leads me away from the window and says, "You shouldn't talk to him. He doesn't have correct manners."

The prince rushes around to block our way. He curtsies, holding out his arms as if he's holding up a skirt. With mischief in his eyes he says, "Sally has *perfect* manners. If you're nice to her, she'll sew you a pair of slippers. Anything to please," the boy says with clear contempt.

"Why shouldn't I try to please them? I'm grateful for all they've done for me—and you should be, too, instead of complaining all the time," she says in a stern voice.

The prince just scowls and turns away from Sally. He pretends to look out the window, but I can tell that he's watching us in the reflection of the glass.

Sally knows, too, so she spins us around and quickly leads me to the opposite side of the room. I glance over my shoulder to see whether the prince is following us but he has taken the girl's place on the window seat. He gazes out the window as if he has forgotten we even exist.

"Is Sally your real name?" I ask.

"You can call me Sarah or Sally—or Etta. I have lots of different names." She pulls me close and confides, "A girl like me has to play many different roles."

"Like an actress?"

She nods and smiles at me. We've only known each other for a couple of minutes, but Sally pulls me close and touches her head to mine as if we're old friends. It's rude to stare so I steal quick glances at the fine lines etched on her cheeks. I know people in Africa sometimes scar their faces to show they belong to a particular tribe.

"Are you from Africa? The prince told me he's from Abyssinia."

"His father was a traitor," she whispers in my ear. "My father was a chief. That's why I have these," she explains tracing a finger over the lines on her cheeks. "Everyone in the royal family is marked that way. That's how they found me."

"Who found you? Were you lost?" I ask.

"Oh no, my dear! I was captured by savages."

I frown and put a bit more space between us. Aunt Joss says Europeans used to call Africans "savages" just because they dressed differently and had different beliefs. If Sally was born in Africa, why would she use that word to describe her own people? I try to get Sally to tell me more.

"What kind of savages?" I ask.

"Fierce warriors! They burned our village and killed my father and mother." She shudders and grips my arm. "It was terrible. I was taken away as a captive. The daughter of a chief is valuable to the king of Dahomey. They would have sacrificed me with all the other captives but Captain Forbes saved me." Sally puts a hand on her chest and sighs dramatically. "He was such a noble man!"

"How did he save you?"

"He told King Ghezo that the great Queen of the Whites would never kill an innocent child. Which is true—Queen Victoria is very fond of children, having nine of her own!"

Victoria? I thought the Queen's name was Elizabeth. I want Sally to keep telling her story so I say, "I bet you were glad King Ghezo decided to let you live."

Sally gives me a solemn nod. "He spared my life and told Captain Forbes to give me to the Queen of the Whites as a gift. That's how I came to live in England as a ward of the Queen. I am her goddaughter and, in a way, her protégé."

I'm not sure what that means but I don't have time to ask any questions before Sally continues her story.

"I lived for a year with dear Captain Forbes and his family until my health took a turn and the Queen sent me to the Missionary School in Sierra Leone."

Sally pulls a lacy handkerchief from inside her sleeve and holds it up to her nose. "That was a trying time for me. Once again I was taken from those I love and forced to rely upon the kindness of strangers. Of course, being the ward of the Queen gave me a certain distinction. I had my own room at school and a private French tutor."

"You speak French?"

Sally must see how impressed I am because she responds, "Bien sûr, mon amie! It is an essential part of any young lady's education. One is not truly accomplished until one can communicate fluently in both English and French."

I'm learning Spanish at school but don't think the few phrases I know would impress Sally. So instead I ask, "What language did you speak before—with your family in Africa?"

The smile vanishes from Sally's face and her eyebrows draw closer together. Her scowl isn't as bad as my low-down-mean-and-nasty look, but it's close. I wonder what I've said to make her mad.

"I have no recollection of those years," she says finally.

"You must remember your own name," I insist.

Sally shakes her head and loosens her grip on my arm.

"You can't have forgotten everything about your life in Africa. That song you were singing didn't sound like English or French."

Sally turns her face away from mine. Then she pulls her arm

free and heads toward the door. "I have to go now...Princess Alice is waiting for me."

If a girl I'd just met in Brooklyn acted that way, I'd say, "Fine, *be* like that." I don't need any fair-weather friends. But I'm not in Brooklyn and I don't want to be left alone in this creepy castle. I'm about to go after Sally when I hear a voice behind me.

"She always does that."

I spin around and find a different boy running his fingers along the grand piano's ivory keys. A closer look confirms that it's still the prince but he has aged—again. Now the prince looks like he's about my brother's age. His woolen suit has been replaced with a fancy velvet one, and his curly hair has grown long enough to be parted on the side.

"Are you going somewhere?" I ask, thinking perhaps that would explain his formal clothes.

"No," he replies testily. "Where would I go?"

I jump when the prince suddenly slams his hands on the piano keys. In those clothes he looks like a little prince but his eyes are flashing with rage.

"Temper, temper," chides Sally. "You know they don't like it when you're angry."

"I don't care!" cries the prince defiantly.

Sally just makes a disapproving sound with her tongue before turning away and gliding through the wall.

Once she's gone, the prince seems to calm down. He sinks onto the cushioned piano bench and stubbornly stabs the same key over and over.

"What did she tell you about my father?"

I think back to what Sally said and decide it's best not to share. "Not much," I assure him. "Do you remember your parents?"

"Of course, I remember them! My father was a noble man—*not* a traitor and *not* a coward. He stood up to the British and then took his own life rather than surrender. The British soldiers... they went into our home and took everything. Everything of value they could lay their hands on—including me."

I frown as I imagine what it would be like to watch strangers loot my home. Then I think of how awful it would be to lose my father at the same time.

"What about your mother?" I ask as gently as I can.

"She died on the way to the coast," he whispers before biting his lip to stop it from trembling.

The prince stops pressing the piano key and silence fills the room. I creep forward until I am standing next to the piano. When he still says nothing, I sit on the edge of the bench with my back to the keys. Sometimes when you need to cry, you don't want to be alone but you also don't want someone watching you.

The prince sniffles and pulls a neatly folded kerchief from the inside pocket of his velvet jacket. He dabs at his eyes and nose before continuing.

"Sally says I should be grateful, but I'm not! I didn't *ask* to be brought to this cold, gloomy island. Some people do try to be kind, but mostly they just stare and say rude things about my color. There's no point trying to fit in. I just want to go home!"

The prince flings his arm across his eyes and collapses against the piano. I feel my own eyes filling with tears and wonder what I should say or do to make him feel better. I turn a little toward him and place a tentative hand on his heaving back. When he doesn't respond, I rub his back the way Mama does when I'm really upset. After a while, the prince stops sobbing and sits up once more.

"Why stay here if you're so unhappy?" I ask.

The prince gets up and wanders over to the window. Then he shrugs hopelessly and gazes out the rain-streaked window. "This is my final resting place," he says solemnly and then adds, "I'm so, so tired."

We both jump when a grandfather clock in the room begins to chime. The prince surprises me by spinning around and grabbing my hand.

"You should go," he says with sudden urgency.

I open my mouth to object but then realize he's right. I don't know how long I've been gone, but Aunt Joss must be worried about me. So I follow the prince as he opens the secret door in the wall and guides me down the dark corridor once more.

We emerge in the same State Apartment where we first met. The prince lets go of my hand and watches as I climb back over the rope divider. When I'm standing with the other tourists, I look at the prince standing in the luxurious room by himself and feel a sudden stab of pain in my chest. I don't want to leave him on his own.

He must see the tears shining in my eyes because he says, "Watch this," with a mischievous grin. "They don't see me but I still make my presence known."

The prince walks over to a stern-faced castle warden who's standing next to the doorway that connect one room to another. Then he winks at me uses his finger to nudge a large painted vase closer and closer to the edge of the mantelpiece.

At first the warden doesn't believe his eyes, but then the prince gives the vase one last poke, it wobbles and falls off the mantelpiece! The warden gasps and dives for the vase, tripping over the red rope but managing to catch the priceless antique before it hits the ground and shatters.

Sally would disapprove and call the prince a "naughty boy," but I can't help laughing at his prank. Another warden rushes over to help her colleague disentangle himself from the red rope wrapped around his legs. They restore the vase to its place on the mantel and urge visitors to keep moving.

"I'd better go find my aunt," I tell the prince. "Thank you for the private tour of the castle and...and for sharing your story with me."

I want to say more but suddenly I feel a hand on my shoulder. I look up and see Aunt Joss smiling down at me.

"There you are!" she cries. "Done with those sketches yet?"

I quickly try to come up with a believable excuse to explain my long absence. But then I take a good look at Aunt Joss and realize she's not upset at all! She hasn't reported me lost to the castle wardens, and she doesn't even seem to realize that I've been gone for over an hour.

"I'm starving," she says with one hand on my shoulder and another on her rumbling stomach. "Let's head over to the chapel and see if we can find Winston and your mum. We can always finish touring the castle this afternoon."

I nod and let Aunt Joss steer me out of the room. When I look back over my shoulder, the prince is gone.

7.

Aunt Joss runs into an old professor friend as we're leaving the State Apartments. They're so busy catching up that they don't notice me scanning every corner of the castle as we head toward St. George's Chapel. I don't want to miss a chance to glimpse the prince or Sally one more time. My eyes are so wide open that Winston gives me a funny look when we finally reach the chapel.

"Are you okay?" he asks. "You look like you've seen a ghost."

"That's because I have!" I whisper.

Aunt Joss introduces Mama to her friend and the three of them start debating where to have lunch. I pull Winston aside and tell him about the ghosts in the castle.

"Are you sure they were dead?" he asks.

"They walked through walls and closed doors," I tell him.

"Definitely ghosts," Winston concludes. "I wish I'd stayed with you instead of waiting in line to see the dolls' house. Think we can go back to the State Apartments?"

"I'm not sure they're still inside the castle," I tell him. "Sally seems to come and go as she pleases, and the prince said he was tired."

Winston thinks for a moment. "Ghosts don't experience

fatigue the way humans do, but if they're restless that usually means something about their life is unfinished."

"He wants to go home, I know that much," I say. "The prince also said something about his final resting place."

Suddenly Winston's face lights up. "That's it!" he cries. "Was he really a prince? I mean, are you sure he was royalty?"

"That's what he said," I reply. "Prince Alemayehu of Abyssinia."

"That's the historical name for Ethiopia," Winston tells me.

"Well, I didn't ask for proof but he definitely had a regal air about him," I conclude.

"Important people aren't always buried in cemeteries like regular people." Winston pauses to point at the chapel behind us. "Sometimes they're buried *inside* the church."

A shiver goes up my spine. I take a good look at the chapel, which seems more like a cathedral to me. "How can someone be buried *inside* a church?"

"There could be a crypt in the basement, or remains can even be interred—buried—just under the floor. If there's a stone effigy—a likeness of the dead person—then the remains are usually in the sarcophagus directly underneath it."

"You know an awful lot about graves," I say, though the truth is, Winston knows a lot about everything!

He just shrugs and says, "I wrote an essay last year on comparative burial rituals for my history class. You can tell a lot about different cultures by how they treat their dead."

I think about that for a moment. Then I pull out my green visitor information pamphlet, which lists important facts about

Windsor Castle and its residents. "If kings and queens have lived here for almost a thousand years, how many of them are buried in the chapel?" I ask.

Winston whistles and scans the pamphlet, too. "Hard to say, really, but my guess would be *a lot*!"

When we don't find Prince Alemayehu's name listed in the pamphlet, I shove it in my back pocket. The three adults are still discussing the dining options in town so I tug at Winston's arm and whisper, "Let's go!"

We try to slip away unnoticed but Mama stops us in our tracks by saying, "Where are you two sneaking off to?"

"We just want to see the chapel," I tell her in my most innocent voice.

But Mama shakes her head. "It's time for lunch, Zaria. Why don't we find somewhere to eat first? We'll come back and tour the rest of the grounds later this afternoon."

"We're not hungry," Winston insists. "And we won't be long—we promise. We're on a quest!"

Aunt Joss raises one eyebrow. "What kind of quest?"

"An educational one," I assure her. "There's an African prince buried inside the chapel."

Mama and Aunt Joss look surprised but her professor friend nods at us. "You're almost right," he tells us. "There's a marker for Prince Alemayehu in the nave but he's not actually buried inside."

"Can't we go see it? Please, Mama. We won't be long, I promise."

Aunt Joss sighs and says, "Far be it from me to interfere with an educational quest. Dorette, why don't you stay with them?

Marvin and I will go into town and find a place for us to have lunch. I'll text you if we find anything decent."

Mama gives Aunt Joss a tired nod and follows us over to the chapel. As soon as we get inside, I see an elderly White woman sitting on a bench. She looks like somebody's grandmother except she's wearing a billowy red gown like the kind students wear at graduation.

"Excuse me," I say, "can you tell us where the prince is buried?"

"There are several princes buried here at St. George's. Which one did you have in mind?" she asks with a smile.

"He's from Africa," I tell her. "His name is Prince Alemayehu."

The steward's eyes light up. "Oh, yes! Our Ethiopian prince. You'll find a plaque dedicated to him in the nave next to the Urswick Chantry. Here—I'll show you."

Mama sinks down onto the bench as the steward gets to her feet. "I'll wait for you here," she says. "Don't take too long. We don't want to keep Aunt Joss waiting."

The steward moves briskly, her thick rubber-soled shoes making no sound at all as she walks down the stone aisle. Folding chairs arranged in rows fill the center of the nave, forcing us to go around. A large stained-glass window lets in what little light there is on such a gloomy day.

Finally we stop at a brass plaque attached to the wall in a far corner of the chapel.

"Here we are," says the steward. "His is a sad story—he died so young and so far from home. But I do love this final line, 'I was a stranger and ye took me in.' That's taken from the Bible—the book of Matthew, I believe."

It doesn't take long for us to read the handful of words engraved on the shiny plaque:

Near this spot

lies buried

ALAMAYU

the son of

Theodore

King of Abyssinia:

Born 23 April 1861

Died 14 November 1879

This tablet placed

here to his memory

by Queen Victoria

I was a stranger

and ye took me in.

Beneath the prince's name is a line written in a language I don't recognize. The steward says it's the prince's name written in Amharic, which is the official language of Ethiopia. Below that, a silver plate has been attached to the original brass plaque. It reads,

VISIT OF H.I.H. TAFARI MAKONNEN, REGENT OF THE EMPIRE AND HEIR TO THE THRONE OF ETHIOPIA JULY 1924

"What does H.I.H. stand for?" I ask the steward.

"His Imperial Highness. A few years later that gentleman became Haile Selassie I, the last Emperor of Ethiopia. He was also made a Stranger Knight—a member of the Order of the Garter—in 1954."

I look at the bible verse on Prince Alemayehu's brass plaque. "Why did they make him a *stranger* knight?" I ask.

"Because he's not British," Winston replies.

The steward nods. "The Order of the Garter is one of the oldest and highest honors in England. Monarchs from other countries are sometimes invited but Emperor Selassie was, I believe, the only one from Africa."

I look at the other markers and tombs that surround the prince's small plaque. The grand memorial to Princess Charlotte has marble angels and veiled mourners weeping at her feet. A statue of King Leopold I stands nearby.

"So…is the prince buried somewhere around here?" I ask.

"Yes, dear," the steward replies. "Queen Victoria arranged for him to buried outside the chapel, I believe."

Winston turns his head so the steward can't hear him mumble, "So much for 'taking him in.'"

We thank the steward for her help and she smiles warmly at us before briskly walking away. For a moment Winston and I simply stare at the shiny plaque. At the top there is a cross and a lion wearing a crown within a circle. At the bottom, in another circle, is St. George slaying the dragon.

Winston points at the two circles. "That's the patron saint of England and the lion of Judah," he tells me.

For once, I don't ask Winston to explain. I just shiver and look around the nave with its soaring columns, vaulted ceiling, tomb-lined walls, and cold tile floor.

"I hate to think that this is the prince's final resting place," I say.

"It's not, really, if he's buried outside," Winston reminds me.

I shiver again and then hear a strange rustling sound coming toward us.

Winston looks up and says, "Is there a wedding here today? That lady's awfully dressed up. She looks like a bride."

I follow Winston's gaze and to my surprise see Sally coming towards us! She's all grown up now and wears an elegant gown that sweeps the stone floor as she gracefully glides toward us.

I turn to Winston, amazed. "You can see her?" I ask.

"Sure—can't you?" he replies.

"Yes, but—can anyone else see her?"

We look around but no one in the chapel seems to notice the regal Black woman in the silk dress. "You look lovely," Winston says, his eyes shining with admiration.

Sally nods to acknowledge his compliment and says, "I was married in this dress."

"Here in St. George's Chapel?"

Sally shakes her head. "I was married to Captain James Davies in the Church of St. Nicholas at Brighton. Despite the rain it was a splendid affair!"

"I'm sure it was," Winston says with a sigh. He's clearly smitten and Sally seems to expect and enjoy the attention.

She reaches out a gloved hand and touches Winston's cheek. Looking at him but speaking to me, Sally says, "Your friend has much better manners than the prince."

"This is Winston," I tell her, "and my name is Zaria. We're so glad to see you!"

"Are you a princess?" Winston asks, his eyes wide with awe.

Sally smiles graciously and says, "That word was never used by my people, but I am of royal blood."

I suddenly remember how my conversation ended with the other Sally—the younger one. I clear my throat and say, "Uh—I'm sorry if I offended you before. I just wanted to know more about you. You've had such an interesting life."

"Ah, but what are my tales worth, in the end," Sally says with a sigh. She traces her gloved fingertips over the words etched on the prince's brass plaque. "My husband built a monument to me in Western Lagos."

"Lagos? That's in Nigeria!" cries Winston.

Sally nods. "My husband was a prosperous businessman. He owned a cocoa farm there."

"Is that where you…I mean, did you…pass away there?" I ask as delicately as I can.

Sally shakes her head and begins to slowly walk away. Winston and I try to follow her but the poofy skirt of her fancy dress gets in the way. Finally we dodge around her and walk in front so we

New Yo

can hear the rest of her story.

"My life ended on another island—Madeira in Portugal. The doctors thought the climate would soothe my lungs, but there was nothing more they could do. Still, I have some fond memories of that place and enjoy visiting now and again."

"I've been wondering," I say, choosing my words carefully, "how you manage to travel from place to place when the prince seems stuck here at the castle."

Sally nods thoughtfully but says nothing for a long while. Finally she sighs and says, "Sorrow binds him to this place. Sorrow and rage are links in the same awful chain."

Sally turns and heads back toward the corner where the prince's plaque is displayed. Her graceful form seems to float over the tiles beneath our feet. Winston and I scramble to get in front of her again without seeming to lead (which would be disrespectful).

"I told you before that Captain Forbes was like a father to me. I was heartbroken when he died, and I grieve for him still. And, of course, I also mourn my dear parents who lost their lives to war. The prince has never stopped grieving for all he has lost—his parents, his homeland. He remembers too much and yet...not enough."

It feels like Sally is speaking in riddles. I look at Winston to see if her words make sense to him, but he looks just as confused.

"I've tried to advise him but he won't listen to me. I fear he sees me as his enemy or his rival, but I am neither. Perhaps..."

Sally's voice trails off as she stares intently at the words etched on the prince's plaque.

"Yes?" I ask, hoping she'll continue.

Sally tears her eyes away and places one hand on my shoulder and the other on Winston's.

"Perhaps you two could share with him a lesson I learned in my travels."

"Sure," I say, eager to find a way to help the lonely prince. "What should we tell him?"

Sally bends and looks into our faces. "He and I were torn from our homes when we were about your age. Tell him…tell Prince Alemayehu to hold onto that which binds him to home."

That sounds like another riddle! I want to check with Winston but find myself unable to tear my eyes away from the African princess.

"We think that we come from a place that can be marked on a map. But countries do not create us—we are shaped by our attachments. We come from love. You must help the young prince to remember this."

Somehow Winston manages to break the spell that Sally seems to have cast over us.

"How can we do that?" he asks respectfully.

Sally removes her hands from our shoulders and clasps them in front of her. She straightens and confidently says, "I trust you will find a way."

Sally nods, letting us know we've been dismissed. Then she turns and starts to walk away. I look over at Winston and see that his mouth is hanging open, too! There are so many questions I want to ask her but the words stick in my throat. To our surprise—and relief—Sally turns and speaks once more.

"Earlier, you asked my name. When I drew my last breath, I

was Sarah Forbes Bonetta Davies. But I was born with another name. My parents called me Aina. It means 'difficult birth' in Yoruba—a girl child born with the cord around her neck. The cord binds the child to its mother until it is cut. But I left Africa with a another sort of cord that could not be severed—an invisible cord that bound me to my place of birth, my family, my people."

Sally smiles and begins humming the song I heard her singing this morning. Then she wades through the rows of folding chairs in the center of the nave and vanishes before our eyes.

8.

Winston and I don't say much during lunch or on the short drive back to Brixton. Mama and Aunt Joss assume we're just tired and we let them believe it's exhaustion that makes us so quiet. As soon as we get home, Winston and I race up to our room and shove the door over the shag carpet until it closes completely.

"Right," says Winston.

"Right," I repeat. "What are we going to do? We have to help the prince."

"Agreed. But first we have to figure out just what the princess meant."

"Sally trusts us to figure it out."

Winston grins. "I trust us, too! We'll figure out what the prince needs and then ask our mums to take us back to the castle."

"Mama won't leave Pa on his own again," I tell him. "I think she already feels guilty about us going out two days in a row."

"My mum won't mind taking us," Winston assures me. "We're on an educational quest, remember?"

"Then we better get to work," I answer with a grin. I get out my tablet but warn Winston that the internet here isn't great. Pa doesn't have wifi so we have to rely on a nearby hotspot that isn't all that hot.

Winston goes downstairs and asks to borrow his mother's

phone. Using the phone and tablet, we spend the rest of the evening researching Prince Alemayehu and Sarah Forbes Bonetta Davies. The ghosts we met in the castle look just like the photos we find on the internet. Learning more about their lives makes me feel like we really have gone back in time!

"Check out this article," Winston says suddenly.

My eyes are tired so I tell Winston to read it out loud. His eyes quickly scan the online article but no words come out of his mouth. "What does it say?" I ask finally.

Winston frowns. "It says that in 2007, the Ethiopian government asked the Queen to return the prince's remains."

"Remains?"

For a moment, Winston and I frown at each other in silence. I know that dead bodies decompose once they're buried in the ground. The prince died a long time ago—back in 1879. If he really was buried in a brick vault outside St. George's Chapel, then only bones would be left at this point.

"You mean…they wanted the Queen to dig him up? Why?"

"They wanted to give the prince a proper burial in Ethiopia, where he belongs." Winston keeps on reading and his frown deepens. "This article says the Queen is considering the request but that was nine years ago. I can't find anything online proving it actually happened."

I fall back on the bed and close my eyes. "It's so sad," I say quietly.

"What is?" Winston asks.

"Everything that happened to Sally and Alemayehu. They were younger than us when they were taken away from their families and their homes. Just imagine how you'd feel if that happened to you!"

I expect Winston to respond right away but when he stays silent, I prop myself up on my elbows and look at him. He has a funny look on his face.

"What's wrong?" I ask.

Winston shrugs. "Nothing. It's just that...well, I'm adopted."

"I know. But that's not the same as being kidnapped," I say. "Is it?"

"No, it's not," Winston says. "But I think I know how Sally and Alemayehu must have felt when they left one world and entered another. It takes time to adjust and sometimes, even though you want to fit in, people still see you as an outsider. You feel like an imposter, like everyone can tell you don't really belong."

My stomach twists into an uncomfortable knot. "Is that how you feel in our family?" I ask Winston. "I mean, when you're with us?"

Winston thinks for a moment. Then he says, "Vanessa and her sisters will probably never accept me. But when I'm with Mum or with you, I feel like I'm at home," Winston says with a smile, "because I can be myself around you."

I smile back, relieved. "Good. That's how I feel when I'm with you, too. And I think that's how we have to make the prince feel. Sally said she had to play lots of different roles, and I think she tried hard to please other people. But when she sings that song—the one from her childhood in Nigeria—I think she feels most like…like her true self."

"When do you feel most like *your* true self?" Winston asks.

I'm not sure what to say. Then there's a knock at the door and Mama calls out, "Time for bed, you two!"

Winston takes a quick shower but when it's my turn, I run a bath instead. As the tub fills with water and bubbles, I think about Winston's question. When *do* I feel like my true self? Here in London or at home in Brooklyn? When I'm with my family or lost inside one of my books? I soak in the sudsy water until Mama knocks on the bathroom door.

She pops her head in and says, "It's getting late, Zaria."

"I just need a few more minutes, Mama," I say.

Mama opens the door enough to fit half of her body into the tiny bathroom. Her forehead wrinkles the way it always does when she's worried. "What's on your mind?" Mama asks.

I sink a bit deeper beneath the surface of the water. "Home," I tell her.

"Two more days and we'll be back in Brooklyn," Mama says with a smile. "I'm sure you've missed your brother."

I know Mama's just teasing me and I want to smile back but instead I ask, "Who's your true self, Mama? I mean, are you British or American or Caribbean?"

Mama looks surprised. "I don't really think of myself as one or the other," she tells me. "I usually feel like I'm all three, all at once."

"All the time?" I ask.

"Most of the time," Mama says. "When I'm here in London, I feel very American. And sometimes when I'm in New York, I feel very British. Identity's funny that way."

I yawn and accept the towel Mama holds out for me. Winston's already asleep by the time I get back to our room. I turn out the light and slip into bed but for a long time I lie awake in the dark, trying to answer Winston's question.

Mama and Aunt Joss agree to take us to Brixton market the next day so long as we first visit the Black Cultural Archives. I smother a groan—not another museum! But Winston assures me I won't be bored—and he's right. In the BCA's one-room gallery there's an exhibit about Black Britons during the Georgian period—that's the reign of King George III who lost his mind and the thirteen colonies in the American Revolution.

Turns out Black people have been living in England for hundreds and hundreds of years! At the BCA we learn that fifteen thousand Black people lived in England during the Georgian period. Some were enslaved, some were born free. Some were soldiers or sailors, and some were abolitionists working to end the African slave trade. We even learn about a Black boxer from the US who fought matches in England. As I look at the portraits on the gallery walls, I find myself wondering if Sally would have known any of these people.

When I ask Winston he says, "Probably not. The Georgian period ended in 1830 and Sally wasn't born until 1843. That means she belongs to the Victorian era, and so does the prince."

Mama has a funny look on her face. The BCA is brand new, so I don't think she's feeling nostalgic the way she did at the Museum of Natural History. I slip my hand in hers and ask, "What's wrong, Mama?"

She gives my hand a squeeze and blinks a few times before

answering. “Nothing’s wrong, baby,” she says. “I just wish I had learned all of this when I was your age.”

Aunt Joss and Winston join us. “Imagine who we’d be today,” Aunt Joss says softly, “if we only knew.”

“Knew what, Mum?” Winston asks.

“That we’ve been here all along. So when people try to treat us like Johnny-come-lately—or tell us to go back where we came from—we could lift our chins and say, ‘We arrived on this island with the Romans, and we’re not going anywhere.’”

Our family came to England from Nevis, not Rome, but I think I know what Aunt Joss means.

We have delicious roti for lunch in the BCA café. Then it’s time to go shopping! Winston and I would rather go to the market on our own, but Mama and Aunt Joss insist on going with us. And as soon as we reach Electric Avenue, Mama and Aunt Joss start cutting up like they’re teenagers again.

Winston tries not to laugh when his mother starts singing and revving an imaginary motorcycle.

“‘We gonna rock down to Electric Avenue—and then we’ll take it higher!’”

“Out in the street!” Mama sings out.

I know that song and I bet Winston does, too. Whenever she feels homesick for England, Mama pulls out her records and plays songs she used to listen to as a teenager in the ’80s. Some of the songs are pretty good, but I don’t need Mama to give everyone at Brixton Market a live performance of Eddy Grant’s greatest hits right now.

Winston and I look at one another. We’d already planned to

ditch our mothers so we could shop for the prince on our own, but now seems like the perfect moment.

"We're going to look over here," I tell Mama as she keeps on singing and bumps hips with Aunt Joss.

Winston and I rush off without waiting for a response. Aunt Joss calls out, "Stay where we can see you!"

Brixton Market makes me homesick for Brooklyn. In the center of the narrow street, which is closed to cars, stalls offer all kinds of things—colorful dashikis, lacy lingerie, frilly dresses for girls. Vendors sell all kinds of fruits and vegetables, displaying them in silver bowls. A seafood shop has fish and even octopus displayed on beds of ice, and chicken dangle from racks with their feathers gone but their heads still attached. This is the sort of market Mama shops at when she goes over to Church Avenue on Saturday morning.

I'm not sure we're going to find what we're looking for here, but Winston tells me to follow him so that's what I do. When the block ends, we cross the street and keep following the market lane, though there are fewer vendors on this end. Finally that lane ends as well and Winston and I find ourselves in front of the Brixton Recreation Center. There are only a few stalls on this street and some restaurants with open doors that let the mouth-watering smell of Caribbean food waft out into the street.

Winston leads me down to a table covered in the strangest selection of items. There's a clarinet waiting to be assembled, lots of glittering costume jewelry, tarnished war medals, several pairs of sunglasses, and two small metal statues of an owl and a boy riding an elephant. There are also a couple of wooden statues that look like they may have come from Africa.

I pick up the owl and trace my fingertip over its carved feathers. I've never seen an owl in Brooklyn, but they always play an important role in my favorite magical books.

"The owl of Minerva," says Winston. "She was the Roman goddess of wisdom."

"How much?" I ask the vendor.

He rocks his head from side to side and finally says, "£5."

I put the owl back on the table and wrap my hand around the heavy coins in my pocket.

"You're supposed to make a counter offer," Winston whispers in my ear.

"We don't have time to haggle. We're here to find something for the prince," I remind him. "I can shop for souvenirs for myself later."

The vendor is wearing a baseball cap and has his hands jammed in the pockets of his jeans. "Looking for something in particular?" he asks. His voice has an accent that isn't British.

I can't exactly say, "We're shopping for a ghost," so I quickly think of something else to say. "Uh…we're looking for something—anything—from Ethiopia."

"I am from North Africa," the man tells us.

"Morocco?" guesses Winston.

"Algeria," the man replies with a smile. "I have some things here from different parts of Africa but nothing from Ethiopia. You should try the shop across the street—the owner is from Addis Ababa."

"That's the capital of Ethiopia," Winston tells me.

We thank the vendor and cross the street. The red awning above the store has the same kind of writing as the plaque in St. George's Chapel. We can't read the Amharic words, but in the window of the shop we see beautiful shirts with embroidered collars and racks displaying jewelry that looks way outside our budget. Winston tries to enter the shop but the door is locked. A sign on the door tells shoppers to ask for the owner in a nearby café.

We find the café a few doors down and go inside. The smell of coffee greets us, reminding me that Mama's favorite coffee comes from Ethiopia. Only a few people are in the café but they all stop talking and turn to stare at us. This time I let Winston speak for the two of us since he sounds like a local and not like a tourist.

"Hello," he says politely. "We'd like to buy something from the shop next door."

A woman standing at the cash register comes around the counter and nods at us. Without saying another word, we follow her out of the café and back to the shop. She unlocks the door with a key worn around her neck on a long piece of string. Then she holds the door open and waits for us to enter.

There are so many things in the store that I don't know where to look first. There are colorful woven baskets and a rack packed tight with clothes made with vibrant African fabric. I finger some of the bead necklaces and try not to look shocked by the prices on the tags. Winston and I don't have a whole lot of money so I keep looking for something priced within our budget.

"What are those?" I ask the shop owner.

"These are shamma cloths," she says. "Both women and men in Ethiopia wear them."

I turn to Winston and whisper, "The prince was wearing something like that when I first saw him in the moat garden!"

Winston steps forward and fingers the beautifully embroidered border of one of the shamma cloths. Gold thread glitters in the sunlight streaming through the window, making the plain white cloth seem fancy enough for a prince.

"Purple is the color for royalty," Winston tells me.

"In Ethiopia or in England?" I ask.

"Hmm, good question," he says. "The Ethiopian flag has three colors: red, gold, and green."

I check the other folded cloths and find one that has a wide strip of purple and narrower bands of red, gold, and green. This cloth seems to have even more gold in it than the first one. I carefully pull it out and show it to Winston.

"Do you think a shamma like that might help the prince's spirit return to his home?" he asks somewhat skeptically.

"It's worth a try," I say. "How much is this one?" I ask the storeowner.

She rolls her lips together and considers the cloth we're holding. "That one is £30."

I look at Winston. Together we have about £33 but we hoped to get more than one gift for the prince. Winston decides to haggle with the shop owner.

"Fifteen," he says confidently, taking the cloth from me.

The shop owner shakes her head but there's a smile on her face. "That cloth was woven by hand in Ethiopia, not made in a

factory in China."

Winston shrugs and hands the beautiful wrap back to the shop owner. I want to ask him what he's doing but decide I'd better play along.

The shop owner takes the cloth but instead of folding it up again she spreads it out so we can see how big it is. "Look at the quality," she says.

"We can't afford it," Winston tells her. "We need to buy three gifts, not just one."

The woman ignores him and turns to me. She drapes the soft cloth over my shoulders and turns me to face a long mirror on the wall. "See? You can wear it as a wrap. Very beautiful," she says with a smile.

I'm ready to hand over the thirty pounds but Winston won't give up. "Fifteen pounds," he says.

The shop owner shakes her head and unwraps me. This time she does fold the shamma cloth up as if she's ready to put it away.

"Twenty," says Winston.

"Twenty-five," counters the shop owner. "You can also choose one of these necklaces, if you like."

She points to a selection of crosses dangling from leather ropes. These crosses aren't like the skinny ones I see people wearing in the US. These crosses are thicker and all four sides are the same length. I pick one out and turn to Winston. "What do you think?"

"Maybe we should get something that smells nice," he suggests. "Certain scents can trigger memories. Lavender always makes me think of my grandmother because she used lavender-scented lotion on her hands."

Winston's never mentioned his grandmother before, but I'm glad he shared this memory from his "other world." The shop owner points to a wooden rack on the counter that holds dozens of small glass bottles filled with scented oil. I put the necklace back and turn the bottles so I can read their labels.

"Which one is the oldest?" I ask the woman. "We need something that people might have used over a hundred years ago."

The woman nods and selects a bottle from the top shelf of the rack. She hands it to me and Winston comes over to take a closer look.

"Frankincense and myrrh?" he says with surprise.

I'm surprised, too. "That's what the Three Kings gave to baby Jesus in the nativity story," I say.

"Along with gold," Winston reminds me, "but this looks a lot more affordable."

"Myrrh and frankincense have been used to heal, cleanse, and protect for thousands of years," the woman tells us.

Winston nods and I set the bottle of oil on the counter next to our shamma cloth. In the corner of the store are round bins full of different colored spices. They all smell good to me—I love Ethiopian food—but how do we know which one to choose? Then my eyes fall on several clear bags stacked next to the spices.

"What are those?" I ask the woman, weighing one of the bags in my hand.

"Kolo," says the shop owner. "It's a popular snack in Ethiopia—roasted chickpeas, barley, and sunflower seeds. For people living here, it's a little taste of home."

She comes over and takes the bag from me. "Here—I give you all three for £22."

"Twenty," says Winston in a surprisingly firm voice.

The woman nods and puts our items into a plastic bag. We hand her our money and thank her before taking our purchases and leaving the store.

"You were pretty good back there," I say once we're back in the street.

Winston grins at me. "Haggling is an art in many countries. Some vendors are offended if you don't try to bargain with them."

"I think the prince will like our gifts," I say with more confidence than I actually feel.

Winston shrugs. "He doesn't have to *like* them, really. They just need to trigger the memories that will take him back home."

Just? I look down at the light bag swinging from my hand and hope we've chosen wisely.

Mama and Aunt Joss are waiting for us at the corner. As soon as we reach them Winston says, "I'll be right back," and dashes off.

I show Mama and Aunt Joss what we bought at the Ethiopian store and a moment later, Winston races back. Breathing hard, he presses something into my hand. I look down and see the owl from the Algerian man's table.

"You'll be going home soon, too," Winston says without looking me in the eye.

I fold the little owl in my hand and press my lips together. I can't really speak right now but at least I manage to smile so Winston knows how grateful I am.

9.

Winston was right! When we tell Aunt Joss we need to go back to Windsor Castle for educational reasons, she agrees to drive us over in the afternoon. Mama stays at home with Pa, and during the drive Winston and I make a plan. We decide to check the State Apartments first before looking for the prince in St. George's Chapel. Winston says it's probably not worthwhile to check Queen Mary's Dolls' House, and I agree.

We get our tickets and dash off with Aunt Joss warning us not to run. We peer over the moat wall but there's no one walking along the path in the garden below. And after spending more than an hour searching every stately room, we exit the castle without catching a glimpse of the prince.

"I wonder if Sally went back to Madeira," I whisper so Aunt Joss can't hear.

"Maybe she's in the chapel again," Winston suggests. "Let's go check the prince's final resting place."

I tell Aunt Joss that we need to visit the chapel next. She follows us over to the lower ward while talking on her phone. "Marvin and his husband are going to meet us for tea afterward," she tells us after hanging up, "so don't be too long."

"You can't rush a quest, Mum," Winston reminds her.

"That's true," Aunt Joss admits as she sits down on the bench by the entrance to the chapel.

Winston and I head inside on our own to find the prince. We start at the most obvious place—the corner where Queen Victoria had the brass plaque installed. When we don't find the prince there, Winston and I leave the nave and inspect the curved garter stalls. Behind each carved wooden seat are brass plates showing the members' coat of arms. Overhead, colorful banners hang from the ceiling.

"Do knights really sit here?" I ask Winston, imagining men in armor squeezing themselves into the narrow stalls.

"Only when the Order of the Garter meets," he explains. "It used to be for real knights and barons but now it's just an honor reserved for the Royal Family and other important people. The annual Garter Ceremony was held here last month, I think. Haile Selassie must have a plate somewhere above one of these stalls."

That sounds interesting but I decide we'd better search for the prince instead. Winston and I leave the stalls behind and walk around the rest of the chapel. We search behind marble statues and peer through locked iron gates but find no trace of Sally or the prince.

As we near the exit, my heart starts to sink. This isn't how the prince's story is supposed to end. I imagined we would find him, present him with our gifts, and the prince would magically return to his home in Ethiopia—we'd be heroes! Magical stories are supposed to have a happy ending, but Winston and I will be as miserable as the prince if our quest fails.

I stop in front of a beautiful red door that's covered in gold swirls. It looks like a magic portal made by elves! A metal bolt runs from the top of the arch into the stone at the bottom, splitting the door in two and making it clear the doors aren't easily opened. A passing steward sees the wonder in my eyes and stops to tell us about the mysterious entrance.

"Those doors were built in the thirteenth century," the elderly White man says. "The scrollwork isn't actually gold, but iron. Still very beautiful, don't you think?"

I nod and ask, "What's on the other side of these doors?"

"The Albert Memorial Chapel," he tells me.

"Can we look inside?" Winston asks.

The steward shakes his head. "I'm afraid these doors are reserved for the Queen's private use," he explains before walking away with his red robe billowing around him.

I sink down onto the low stone steps that lead up to the beautiful doors we can't open. Winston sits beside me, setting the bag with the prince's gifts between us.

"What do we do now?" I ask hopelessly.

Winston sighs, puts his elbows on his knees, and rests his head in his hands. "Try again tomorrow?"

"Tomorrow I have tea with Aunt Pru," I remind Winston. "And the day after that I go back to Brooklyn!"

Winston reaches into the bag and pulls out the small bottle of oil.

"What are you doing?" I ask.

"Desperate times call for desperate measures," Winston says solemnly. Then he stands up and pours the oil out onto the chapel's stone floor.

"Winston!" I cry. "You're going to get us in trouble!"

Winston puts the cap back on the bottle and drops it back into the bag. The strong scent of frankincense and myrrh is almost overpowering. Several people walk by and gives us strange looks. Winston rubs the soles of his shoes into the puddle of oil. "Wait here," he tells me. "I'll be right back."

I shift on the stone steps so I'm farther away from the fragrant oil. It feels like an eternity before Winston reappears, breathing hard from his brisk walk around the chapel.

"That should spread the scent," he explains before taking a seat beside me once more.

"Your sneakers are going to reek forever," I warn him.

Winston just shrugs. "It'll be worth it—if it works."

I look one way and Winston looks the other, but the prince still doesn't appear. I don't want to give up but if we don't go outside soon, Aunt Joss will come inside looking for us. Then our quest really will be over.

Suddenly I feel a cold draft of air blowing on my neck. I turn to Winston and see him shiver, too. The red doors behind us haven't opened, but we can tell that someone has definitely arrived! Leaning against the arched doorway is a teenage boy in a smart tweed suit and tie. He holds a familiar boater, which he's twirling between his hands.

"You came back," the prince says shyly with just a hint of a smile.

I jump up and rush over to him, almost daring to throw my arms around him. "You're here! We're so glad to see you. This is my cousin Winston."

The prince sniffs as Winston gets to his feet. "You smell like frankincense and myrrh—the entire chapel does. Why?" he asks.

I snatch up the bag and pull out the shamma cloth and bag of kolo. I'm nervous and excited so too many words tumble out of my mouth.

"We meant to give it to you as a gift but then we couldn't find you and Winston thought you might be drawn to the scent so he stepped in the oil and walked all around the chapel."

"What have you got there?" the prince asks.

Winston opens the bag of kolo and offers some to the prince. "We thought you might like…a taste of home."

The prince reaches into the bag and takes a small handful of the seeds and grains. He lifts his palm to his nose and sniffs. "Berbere," he whispers before tossing the kolo into his mouth. "This is quite tasty," the prince says as he takes a second handful.

Winston nods at me and I spread out the shamma cloth. "We got you this, too," I tell the prince. "You were wearing something like it when I first saw you in the moat garden."

The prince wipes his hand on his pants and reaches for the cloth. He traces the delicate gold thread and says, "My mother had the finest weavers in the country make our clothes."

Winston and I exchange glances. He nods at me as if to say, "You go first." I take a deep breath and hope the prince won't get upset or vanish when I tell him about Sally.

"Yesterday we came to the chapel. We were admiring your plaque when Sally stopped by." I pause and wait to see if the prince will respond. He just keeps on munching on kolo, so I continue. "She had a message for you. She wanted you to know—

to remember—that we don't only come from places. We come from love."

"That's a strange message," the prince says. "What does it mean?"

I turn to Winston. The look on my face says, "Your turn!"

"Well," Winston begins, "perhaps she meant that your story doesn't start with sadness and loss."

"And if you hold onto the love you knew at the very beginning of your life," I add, "maybe you could roam the way Sally does. She goes everywhere!"

"That's true," the prince says. "I've often wondered how she manages to come and go so easily."

"Sally told us that pain can bind you to a place," I tell the prince. "So if you want to be free, maybe you should try focusing on something else," I suggest.

"Such as?" the prince asks.

"Tell us about your mother," Winston says politely.

The prince sits on the top step and leans back against the red doors. Winston and I sit on a lower step to show respect.

"My mother was a pious woman—very devout. She was going to enter a convent but then she married my father and had me."

The prince stops and sorrow passes over his face like a shadow.

"She must have loved you very much," I say, hoping the prince will go on.

"She did," the prince says with a sad smile. "My mother could trace her lineage all the way back to King Solomon and Makeda, Queen of Sheba. Mother told me lots of stories, but the legend of Makeda was my favorite."

The prince takes another handful of kolo and munches quietly with a small smile on his face. Winston urges the prince to keep talking about the happy times he spent with his mother.

"Can you tell us about Makeda?"

The prince nods eagerly and sits up straight. His face becomes animated and he waves his hands for effect as he talks. I imagine his mother did the same when telling stories to her beloved son.

"Once there was a fierce dragon named Awre. It was a giant horned serpent with fiery eyes and it terrorized the ancient kingdom of Axum. The beast devoured over a thousand animals a day but still was not satisfied. Once a year it demanded that a beautiful maiden be given as tribute. When it was Makeda's turn to be sacrificed to Awre, brave Makeda grabbed the beast by its horn and cut off its head! The people were so grateful they made her Queen of Axum.

"When the queen heard of the wisdom of King Solomon from a trader, she led a caravan of camels laden with gold, jewels, and spices to Jerusalem. She asked the king many questions so that he would share his knowledge with her. Makeda was beautiful, brave, and wise—just like my mother."

Winston and I say nothing while the prince is speaking, but we both notice that he has started to change. First he becomes the younger boy in the velvet suit, and then he shrinks further, becoming the boy in the woolen suit that I first saw in the State Apartments. By the time he finishes his story, the boy sitting between us on the steps is the same one I first saw in the moat garden yesterday except the young prince no longer looks lonely.

"You've changed," I tell him.

The boy laughs and gathers his white robe around his small body. Winston passes him the bag of kolo and the prince tosses another handful into his laughing mouth.

The red doors behind us remain locked yet I shiver once more as a sudden draft of icy air blows against the back of my neck.

Winston asks, "Do you hear that?"

I listen and hear the familiar sound of Sally's long silk skirt sweeping over the chapel's stone floor. Winston and I jump up and beam at Sally. She stops before us and nods at me and then at Winston.

"I see you have shared my message with the prince." We nod and she goes on.

"Never forget," Sally says in a solemn voice. "The things of this world come and go but love—love endures."

She holds out her hand to the young prince and says in a gentle voice, "Come, child. Rise and walk with me."

The prince looks up into Sally's kind face and smiles. If he remembers how much he disliked Sally's younger self, the boy shows no sign. Instead he wraps our shamma cloth around his shoulders and tucks the bag of kolo under his arm. Then the prince takes Sally's hand and the two ghosts walk away.

Winston and I stand frozen on the steps until Sally and Alemayehu turn a corner and disappear from view. Then we dash down the aisle and peer around the corner only to find that the two ghosts have vanished.

"We did it!" Winston exclaims.

I want to celebrate with him but for some reason, I don't feel particularly heroic. All I feel right now is homesick. I bite my lip but a few tears still run down my cheeks. Winston puts his arm around me and leads me outside. When Aunt Joss sees how miserable I look, she calls her friend and cancels the plans she made.

"Let's have our tea at home," she suggests before giving me a quick kiss on the forehead.

I don't say a word on the drive back to London, but as soon as we get home, I rush upstairs to Pa's room. He's sleeping so I carefully crawl into bed beside him. I don't need to read from one of my books today. Even though Pa probably can't hear me, I rest my head against his chest and tell him all about the ghosts in the castle.

10.

One doorman holds an umbrella over our heads so we don't get wet as we step out of the cab. A second doorman—wearing the same black top hat and long brown coat—holds open the door of the hotel.

"Good afternoon, ladies," he says politely.

Mama thanks him as we walk into the lobby of Brown's Hotel. I'm a little disappointed that we're not having tea at Kensington Palace, but Mama assures me this place is just as nice.

A wall of dark wood with beveled glass windows separates the tea room from the hotel lobby. Mama pops her head into the tea room's open door and spots Aunt Pru. Then she kneels down beside me and smooths my hair for the hundredth time. Aunt Joss bought a home perm at the chemist (that's what they call a drugstore over here), but Mama refused to put it in my hair. Instead she combed my puffs out and gave me two tight, tidy plaits. Aunt Joss suggested we use some of her hair butter so my head smells kind of fruity.

We compromised on my clothes. I agreed to wear a dress (my dark denim jumper) so long as Mama let me wear my sparkly unicorn t-shirt underneath. For me, a skirt plus sparkles means I'm dressed up, but I can tell Mama's worried that Aunt Pru won't be impressed.

Mama kisses me on the cheek. "Remember your manners," she says with an anxious smile.

I smother a sigh and wonder what Winston's doing right now. Probably something that's a lot more fun than having tea in this fancy hotel with Aunt Shrew!

I give Mama a quick hug and promise to be on my best behavior. "Are you sure you can't stay?" I ask even though I already know the answer.

"Not this time," Mama says as she stands up. She picks some lint off my jumper and pushes me toward the entrance to the tea room. "Try to have fun, Zaria. Aunt Pru just wants to get to know you better, so be yourself. I'll be back in an hour."

I take a deep breath and walk into the tea room. The first thing I notice is the grand piano. The second thing I notice is that not everyone's dressed up—a couple of people are even wearing jeans! Not Aunt Pru, of course. She's wearing a long-sleeved dress that has crisp pleats on the bottom and ruffles at the cuff and neck. It's a damp, rainy day but Aunt Pru's hair is pressed straight and pulled back into a tight, tidy bun. Even though she's older than Pa, Aunt Pru has hardly any wrinkles. Only the streaks of grey in her hair show her age. The mirror on the wall assures me that I look "neat and tidy," but somehow I feel frizzy and rumpled compared to Aunt Pru.

A woman standing behind a podium gives me a funny look. I run a hand over my too-tight braids and tug at the strap of my jumper. Then I clear my throat and say a bit too loudly, "I'm here to see my aunt." I nod in Aunt Pru's direction since it's rude to point.

The woman smiles and says, "Oh, yes—Ms. Hanley's expecting you. Right this way, miss."

I could have walked over to Aunt Pru by myself but I let the woman lead me to her table. Aunt Pru is seated on a comfortable sofa—at least it could be comfortable with all those cushions, but Aunt Pru is sitting up straight. A menu rests on the low table before her. I'm not sure if I should sit beside her or in the armchair on the other side of the table.

Aunt Pru glances at her watch and says, "You're late, young lady."

That settles it. I slip into the armchair instead of sitting next to Aunt Pru.

"Sorry…traffic," I mumble while opening the tall menu. I try to hide behind it but still feel Aunt Pru's eyes on me. I search for something else to say. "Mama said she'd be back in an hour."

"Then we'd better go ahead and order," Aunt Pru says. A smiling waiter appears out of nowhere. Aunt Pru snatches the menu out of my hands and says, "Tea for two, please."

The waiter nods and disappears with the menu, leaving me alone—with no shield—to face Aunt Pru. I know it's rude to stare but Aunt Pru's eyes are glued on me, so I just stare right back at her. I can last for a whole minute without blinking—just ask my brother. To my surprise, a smile tugs at Aunt Pru's lips.

"You're a bold one, aren't you," she says with what sounds like respect.

"Bold" isn't the same thing as "rude," so I decide to follow Mama's advice and just be myself. "Why did you want to have tea with me, Aunt Pru?"

"Your mother tells me you're an excellent student," Aunt Pru says as she spreads a white linen napkin across her lap.

I do the same with my napkin and think of what to say. I don't want to brag, but I do get straight As at school. "I like to learn," I say simply. "And I really like to read. I might even be a writer when I grow up."

"Is that so?" Aunt Pru leans forward, her eyes brightened by curiosity. "And what will you write?"

"Stories," I tell her. Then I lean forward, too, and add, "Stories full of magic!"

Aunt Pru raises an eyebrow. "What do you know about magic?"

I sit back and drape my arms along the chair's padded armrests. "Oh, I have *lots* of stories to tell." Aunt Pru's family but I'm not sure she'd appreciate hearing about the phoenix on Barkley Street or the ghosts in the castle.

"They say Rudyard Kipling wrote *The Jungle Book* here in this tea room," Aunt Pru tells me.

I look around and try to imagine myself writing a novel while people sip tea and nibble at their finger sandwiches. When I write stories, I usually just lie on my bed with my notebook. I have a hard time focusing when I'm hungry, so I usually keep some snacks hidden under the bed.

I look up and find Aunt Pru scrutinizing me once more.

"Have you read that book?" she asks.

I know my answer will disappoint her, but I tell Aunt Pru the truth just the same. "No, but I saw the movie," I say. "It was pretty good."

Aunt Pru frowns and says, "I fear there may be some…gaps in your education."

I think of the souvenir t-shirts, fridge magnets, and key chains that all say, "Mind the Gap." That's the automated announcement you hear on the Tube warning passengers to step carefully from the train onto the platform. My friend Abena has a gap between her teeth, but I've never noticed a gap in my education.

"The classics still matter," Aunt Pru says and I can tell she's about to say a whole lot more but then the waiter returns, wheeling a cart loaded with food. He sets a three-tier tray on our table and begins describing all the sandwiches and sweets.

My eyes open wide and my stomach starts to rumble. While the waiter sets the rest of our tea things on the table, Aunt Pru tells me to go ahead and eat.

"Pace yourself," she advises. "The scones will come out shortly, followed by the cakes."

There are tiny cakes (the waiter called them "petit fours") on the top plate of the serving tray, but I don't mind if more are on the way! I select a lemon tartlet and try to take a dainty bite instead of shoving the whole thing into my mouth. Aunt Pru pretends to be focused on pouring our tea but I can tell she's still keeping an eye on me.

When I reach for a sugar cube to add to my tea, Aunt Pru softly says, "Use the tongs, please."

That's easier said than done, but I manage to drop the cube into my tea without splashing any on the white tablecloth. I lift the china cup to my mouth and do my best so sip silently. I stick my pinky finger out because that's how British people drink tea on TV.

Aunt Pru hasn't eaten anything yet but I'm too hungry to hold myself back. I've always wanted to try a cucumber sandwich so I pick one from the bottom plate of the serving tray and take a small bite. The cream cheese makes it taste okay but I decide to try a different sandwich next. If there's one thing I've learned on this trip, it's that sometimes the things you read about aren't as exciting—or as tasty—as you thought they'd be!

Aunt Pru finally selects a glass cup filled with chocolate mousse from the top tier. There's a lot of cutlery on the table, but she seems to know exactly which spoon to use.

"Have you enjoyed your time in London?" Aunt Pru asks after dabbing at her mouth with her linen napkin.

I've eaten a lot more food but haven't wiped my mouth yet, so I do the same with my napkin. Aunt Pru nods to show that she approves. I take that as a sign that I can keep on eating! I pick a chocolate éclair from the middle tray and smother a moan of delight as the pastry and cream melt together in my mouth.

"This is the best trip ever," I tell her, rushing to add, "though I'm sorry Pa couldn't go sightseeing with us."

"I understand you read to your grandfather every day," Aunt Pru says in her approving voice.

I just nod since it's rude to talk with your mouth full of éclair. Once I swallow, I wipe my mouth with my napkin again and say, "Aunt Joss doesn't like my books, but I think Pa enjoys the stories I read to him."

Aunt Pru's lips twist as if she's eaten something bitter. "Well," she says, "Jocelyn has always been somewhat…militant in her approach. Does your mother know about your literary

aspirations?"

I feel like Aunt Pru's giving me a vocabulary quiz. "Sure," I tell her. "Mama and I talk about books all the time, and I show her all my stories. Mama wanted to be a poet when she was my age."

"She certainly did," Aunt Pru says with a smile. "But she gave that dream up years ago when she met your father."

Aunt Pru sighs and looks out the window. Mama still writes poems—I know because she shares them with me sometimes. But I don't tell that to Aunt Pru. Instead I slip a cheese and pickle sandwich off the tray and onto my plate.

Aunt Pru takes a sip of tea and then says, "I had high hopes for your mother…once. She, too, was an excellent student—what we used to call 'a credit to the race.' Dorette had a curious mind. I suppose that's what led her to move all the way to America."

Aunt Pru has that disapproving tone in her voice again. I take another bite of my sandwich and keep my eyes on my plate.

Aunt Pru chooses an egg salad sandwich but doesn't take a bite. Instead she says, "My mother always hoped I would grow up to be a nurse, which is a respectable profession, but I felt teaching was my true calling. I taught English for close to forty years. When I retired, the school created a scholarship in my name and invited me to nominate a student of exceptional promise."

Aunt Pru pauses and looks directly at me. I keep my hands in my lap instead of reaching for the pink macaron on the top plate of the serving tray.

"Glenworth is a school with a long, proud history. In recent years they've made a commitment to diversifying the student body and the faculty. I think the headmaster would be delighted to meet you, Zaria. With your academic aptitude and international perspective, you'd be a wonderful addition to the school. You can't become a boarder until you're ten, so you would live with me for a year as a day pupil."

Even though Mama prepared me for this moment, I still don't know what to say. Fortunately the waiter arrives with a plate of scones. I grab the pink macaron and stuff it in my mouth so I won't have to speak for another minute.

Since my mouth is full, I nod when Aunt Pru asks if I'd like more tea. I place the strainer over my cup the way she showed me and then set it in the silver bowl to drain. I use the tongs to add a cube of sugar and pour some milk from the small silver pitcher.

Aunt Pru doesn't press me to respond to her offer. She seems to understand that my silence doesn't mean I'm not grateful. I'm surprised but also relieved when Aunt Pru suddenly starts talking about something else entirely.

"My parents were part of the Windrush generation. Do you know about the *Windrush*?"

I nod and tell Aunt Pru some of what Mama told me yesterday when we visited the Black Cultural Archives in Windrush Square. "It was a ship that sailed from Jamaica to England after World War II. England needed workers and so they welcomed people from their colonies."

"That is correct," Aunt Pru says, "though I'm sure your mother also told you that the welcome mat didn't stay out long."

I nod and take a currant scone from the new plate on the serving tray. Aunt Pru shows me how to cut it crosswise so there's plenty of room to spread raspberry jam and clotted cream. Then she continues her story.

"Bertie—your grandfather—was just a boy when our parents emigrated from the Caribbean, but I was fifteen and done with school. Bertie was left behind with my grandmother but since I was old enough to work, my parents took me with them."

Aunt Pru pauses to brush a stray scone crumb off the white linen tablecloth. "Those were difficult years for our family—and for every family like ours. It didn't matter how polite, or well-dressed, or bright you were. It didn't matter how long or hard you worked at the dirtiest, most menial, low-paying jobs. Even though you sang 'God Save the Queen' alongside them, you weren't welcome because of your accent and the color of your skin. The English needed us, but they didn't want us in 'their' country."

"Did you ever think about going back to Nevis?" I ask.

"I dreamed about going home every night," Aunt Pru tells me. "But there were no jobs and few opportunities back home for a girl like me. I knew I was bright. I just needed a chance to prove myself." Aunt Pru pauses to make sure my eyes are locked on hers. "You deserve that chance, too, Zaria."

For some reason my cheeks start to burn. "I've dreamed about living in England since I was little," I tell Aunt Pru, "and I've always wondered what it would be like to go to a boarding school."

"This is your chance to find out," Aunt Pru says with a smile.

I take a sip of my tea before I reply. "A week ago, I would have been excited about moving to England. But now…"

"Yes?" Aunt Pru waits for me to continue.

"Now I see how important home is. I'm not sure I really

belong here in England. Plus it's not easy being an immigrant—especially when you're just a kid. It wasn't easy for you, was it?"

"No, it wasn't," Aunt Pru admits. "But I like to think that I was able to make it a bit easier for Bertie when he finally joined us in Brixton. And I worked hard to ensure that future generations wouldn't face the same challenges I had to overcome. When you have the courage to open a door, you make it possible for others to walk through after you. I was one of the first West Indian women hired to teach in London schools," Aunt Pru says with pride.

"Then why did you leave?" I ask her.

Aunt Pru sets her tea cup in its saucer without making a sound. "I left shortly after the riot in 1981," she says in a quiet, firm voice. Then Aunt Pru narrows her eyes and looks at me as if she's trying to measure something inside my mind. "Do you know what a riot is, Zaria?"

I think for a moment and say, "'A riot is the language of the unheard.'"

Aunt Pru's eyebrows go up in surprise.

"Martin Luther King said that," I tell her. I take a bite of my scone and leave out the fact that I saw that quote in my brother's essay on the Black Lives Matter movement.

"And what do you think it means?" Aunt Pru asks.

I finish chewing, swallow, and clear my throat. That gives me a bit of time to straighten out my thoughts.

"Well, if people try to tell you how they feel and you don't listen, they'll find another way to get your attention." I've heard Mama and Aunt Joss say something similar plenty of times: "You don't listen, you'll *feel*."

Aunt Pru nods and takes a sip of tea. Then she sighs and says, "Brixton was a very different place then. Despite our striving, the youth—many of them, not all—had lost hope. I taught some exceptional students but even the ones that graduated simply couldn't find work."

Aunt Pru purses her lips and then says, "At that time people were wary of the police. Some officers had abused their authority, so there was no trust between the community and those who were charged with our protection."

"It's like that back home, too," I tell her.

Aunt Pru nods. "Yes, you've had quite a bit of trouble with law enforcement. But then America has always been such a violent place. Wouldn't you like to get away from it all—live someplace more *civilized*?"

My cheeks start to burn again, but this time I know why. "Tell me more about the riot," I say, hoping Aunt Pru can't tell that I'm offended. The United States isn't perfect, but that doesn't mean we're uncivilized!

Aunt Pru looks down at her empty teacup. "A young man was injured and rumors swirled that a police officer was responsible. There was chaos for days—bricks and bottles flying every which way. Looters picking stores clean…fires burning in the middle of the street. Brixton was like a warzone—and your uncle was out there acting like a hooligan."

"Useless?" I say, amazed.

Aunt Pru gives me a stern look but continues telling her story. "Your grandfather felt Eustace was old enough to make his own choices, but I knew better. If the police caught him, he'd end up behind bars or…worse. I went out and dragged Eustace home by his ear! And it's a good thing I did. Look at him now—an esteemed barrister with a successful practice, upholding the law instead of breaking it."

But Uncle Eustace isn't around when Pa needs him, I think to myself. And his daughters…

I don't mean to, but just the thought of snooty Vanessa makes me roll my eyes.

Aunt Pru clears her throat to make sure she has my full attention. "After the riot I decided to leave the chaos of London behind. I was fortunate enough to have a friend who recommended me for a position at Glenworth, and so I made the north of England my home."

Aunt Pru smiles and gazes out the window at the rain-soaked street. "When I was a girl in Nevis, I used to dream about London. All the books I read made it seem like the most important place in the world. But in the end, I found that a quiet life in the country suited me best."

I look out the window, too. This is the rainy weather I hoped for when I first learned we were coming to England. But now that it has been raining for three days straight, I'm missing the clear blue Brooklyn sky.

"I really appreciate your offer, Aunt Pru. But I think that—for now, at least—I belong back in Brooklyn. I miss my family and friends, and all the people and places in our neighborhood. The United States isn't perfect but…well, Brooklyn's where I feel most like my true self."

Aunt Pru's eyebrows go up but not in a disapproving way, so I go on.

"You said before that there are 'gaps' in my education. Maybe you're right. I have a lot to learn about our family, and our history, and…well, I think I should start at home." I watch Aunt Pru to see if she's offended, but she doesn't seem angry or even surprised.

"That sounds like a perfectly reasonable course of action," Aunt Pru says.

I heave a sigh of relief. Then I decide to take a chance and ask, "Can I say one more thing, Aunt Pru?"

"You *may*," Aunt Pru says in her stern English teacher voice. "What is it, child?"

I take a deep breath and sit up straight. "I think Winston would do really well at a school like Glenworth. He's the smartest boy I know and, well, he's part of our family and…he deserves an advantage, too."

Aunt Pru stares at me for a long time. I don't try to outlast her. Instead I reach for another scone and try to slice it the way she showed me. Then I smear jam and clotted cream on it and take a big bite instead of a dainty one. I don't have to try to impress Aunt Pru any more and if she's going to lecture me, I figure I might as well keep on eating.

Finally Aunt Pru says, "Perhaps you're right. Thank you for the suggestion, Zaria."

Now it's my eyebrows that go up in surprise!

Before I can finish my scone, the waiter rolls a cart over that's loaded with different kinds of cake. My eyes open wide—but not my mouth. I'm stuffed!

"Can we take some of this food home?" I ask Aunt Pru.

"Certainly," Aunt Pru replies, "we paid for it." To the waiter she says, "A box, please."

When the waiter returns, I place the remaining treats inside the box and assure Aunt Pru they aren't for me. "Winston can have these for his tea," I tell her.

"You're quite fond of Winston, aren't you?" Aunt Pru asks.

I nod and for a moment think of how much I'll miss Winston when I go home. Then I brighten and says, "He's going to come visit me in Brooklyn next summer." I hesitate but then blurt out, "Maybe Winston could visit you, too."

Aunt Pru smiles. "That's a good idea, Zaria," she says. "It's time I became better acquainted with my nephew."

We head out to the lobby and find Mama waiting for us on a cushioned bench. She jumps up and rushes over to us with an anxious look in her eyes. After giving Aunt Pru a peck on the cheek, Mama asks, "How was tea?"

"Delicious," I tell her, patting my full belly. "Tariq probably would have eaten everything in sight, but I saved some for Winston."

Mama smiles and touches my cheek. "You'll have lots to tell your brother about London when we get home, won't you?"

I surprise even myself by laughing out loud. Heads turn in the hotel lobby and Aunt Pru gives me a disapproving glare.

"I can't wait to get back to Brooklyn," I say as Mama ushers me out the door and into the rainy street. "Tariq will be amazed by the incredible story I have to tell!"

The End

Discussion Guide

1. The Ethiopian government has asked for Prince Alemayehu's remains to be returned. What do you think the Queen should do? Where does the prince truly belong? Write a letter to the Queen expressing your point of view.

2. Learn more about the 1868 British Expedition to Abyssinia. What items were taken from Ethiopia to England? Should museums and monarchs return valuable objects that were taken from other countries long ago? How else can people learn about different cultures in distant places?

3. "Home is where the heart is." What does that mean to you? Is home a place or a feeling you carry in your heart? What objects, foods, scents, or rituals help you feel at home when you're traveling?

4. Dr. Martin Luther King, Jr. once said, "A riot is the language of the unheard." How do you make your voice heard when you're angry or unhappy? Think of an issue or cause that means a lot to you. How would you make others aware of your cause?

5. Sarah Forbes Bonetta Davies had many different names. Do you have a nickname or were you named after anyone? What does it mean to call someone out of their name?

6. Learn more about Sarah's life, starting with her journey from Africa to England on board the *Bonetta* with Captain Forbes. Now write a letter to Aina/Sally/Sarah telling her about a journey you've made. Where do you think she felt most like her true self? Where do you feel most like your true self?

7. Research one Black person from the Georgian period in England. What job did they have? What challenges did they face? What did they contribute to British society? Now watch the first episode of *Back in Time for Brixton* on YouTube: https://www.youtube.com/watch?v=F9B1qevOK8U. What challenges did Caribbean immigrants of the *Windrush* generation face when they first arrived in England? What helped them to feel "at home" even though they were far from "home?"

8. In June 2016 people in the UK voted to leave the European Union. There was also a presidential election in the United States that year. Immigration was an important issue for voters in both elections. How are immigrants treated in your country? Should immigrants be welcomed or turned away? How would your country be different without immigrants?

Acknowledgments

I began researching this book in 2015 but in a way, I really started it as a child in Canada. When I was Zaria's age, I believed magical adventures only happened to White children because the books I read—all set in England—showed only White children casting spells, and solving mysteries, and ultimately saving the day. As an adult, I decided I would "talk back" to those books and create stories where kids who looked like me had the chance to be the hero.

I traveled to London in October 2015 and February 2016 to conduct research for this book. Most of the novel was written long after those trips, however, and so I relied on friends in the US and UK as well as other sources. I read *At Her Majesty's Request: an African Princess in Victorian England* by Walter Dean Myers, and I watched several helpful videos that I found online. I take responsibility for any errors in this novel, though I should point out that *The Ghosts in the Castle* is speculative fiction—my intention was not to educate the reader but to inspire greater curiosity in the past. I hope young readers and the adults in their lives will use this novel and the discussion guide as a starting point for further research.

Photography is not allowed inside Windsor Castle; I tried to take careful notes but I'm grateful for the complete transcript of Prince Alemayehu's plaque provided by Anastasia Porteous, Archives Trainee at St. George's Chapel Archives & Chapter

Library. I set the final chapter of the novel at Brown's Hotel because my friend Prof. Mary Condé kindly treated me to tea there twice; she also sent me the novels of Alex Wheatle when I told her I wanted to learn more about the riots in Brixton. In 2004 I went to Djibouti for five weeks but was unable to visit Ethiopia; my friend Sayida Self gifted me a beautiful shamma cloth before I left, and it matches the one given to the prince by Winston and Zaria. Nancy Vichert, my high school English teacher, still corrects my writing and I appreciate the polish her eagle eye brings to my work. Creator and author Tina Olajide has lived on both sides of "the pond" and her feedback was invaluable. When I needed advice about Ethiopian culture and history, my neighbor Ben Watkins generously shared his expertise with me. I've been fortunate to collaborate on three books with UK illustrator Charity Russell, and she continues to amaze me with her artistic ability--she also informed me of Dippy's retirement! Finally, my friend and fellow writer Kate Foster is always my first reader, and I'm especially grateful for her insight around Winston's adoptee narrative.

I wrote a thousand words a day for most of the month of November, and was inspired by daily news reports coming out of North Dakota. The Standing Rock Sioux and their many allies fought to protect water sources endangered by the Dakota Access Pipeline; their brave resistance helped me find perspective as I wrote this novel and regained my balance following the US presidential election. I have long felt that Blacks in the US and throughout the diaspora have much to learn from Indigenous communities, and I keep this meme on my desktop to remind me of our shared struggle:

exist &
resist &
indigenize &
decolonize

I chose to self-publish this book because I knew the traditional publishing industry wouldn't find value in a story about Black children learning about the legacy of imperialism. Making my own books without waiting for permission is, for me, an act of resistance and I encourage others to do the same. I'm still actively working to decolonize my imagination, and I regularly meet children of color who show me books they've made that only feature White children. I hope my stories will remind all young readers that magic can happy to anyone, anywhere. Everyone benefits when we read, write, and dream in color!

Zetta Elliott
December 17, 2016
Brooklyn, NY

About the Author

Zetta Elliott is the award-winning author of over twenty books for young readers. She lives in Brooklyn and loves castles, tea and scones, and the powerful magic that comes from knowing her history.

Learn more at www.zettaelliott.com

About the Illustrator

Charity Russell lives in Bristol, England with her husband and two children. She has a Master's Degree in Illustration and Design from The University of Sunderland. She loves all things bookish and receiving hand written letters in the post.

www.charityrussell.com

Meet Zaria and her Brooklyn friends in City Kids Book #1!

Best friends Carlos and Tariq love their block, but Barkley Street has started to change. The playground has been taken over by older boys, which leaves Carlos and Tariq with no place to call their own. They decide to turn the yard of an abandoned brownstone into their secret hang-out spot. Carlos and Tariq soon discover, however, that the overgrown yard is already occupied by an ancient phoenix! When the Pythons try to claim the yard for their gang, the magical bird gives the friends the courage to make a stand against the bullies who threaten to ruin their beloved neighborhood.

Travel through time in City Kids Book #2!

Summer vacation has just begun and Dayshaun wants to spend Saturday morning playing his new video game. But Dayshaun's mother has other plans: she volunteers at a nearby community garden and that means Dayshaun has to volunteer, too. When Dayshaun puts on his grandfather's grubby old gardening hat, something unexpected happens—the hands of time turn backward and Dayshaun finds himself in the free Black community of Weeksville during the summer of 1863! While helping the survivors of the New York City Draft Riots, Dayshaun meets a frail old man who entrusts him with a precious family heirloom. But will this gift help Dayshaun find his way back to the 21st century?

CPSIA information can be obtained
at www.ICGtesting.com
Printed in the USA
LVHW01s1345220418
574433LV00004B/674/P

9 781540 357588